'Oof!'

'Oh, God – I'm so sorry!' Megan looked down at the boy lying on the ground. 'I completely didn't see you! Here . . .' She offered him a hand, but the boy pulled himself up, panting.

'Are you blind?' he exclaimed, brushing down his jeans.

Megan felt embarrassed. 'No. I'm sorry, I was in a hurry. Are you all right?'

The boy stared at her. He was taller than Megan, with jet-black hair that looked like it might be dyed. His eyes were a clear pale grey, and his face – well. Megan gulped. He was quite possibly the most good-looking boy she had ever seen, with high, defined cheekbones and dark eyelashes and eyebrows. He looked like a model. 'Who are you?' the boy demanded. 'Are you new here?'

Look out for more

stories!

Star Crossed

Coming soon:
Ice Dreams

sweet
hearts

Strictly Friends?

Jo Cotterill

♥ ♥ ♥ ♥ ♥ ♥ ♥

RED FOX

SWEET HEARTS: STRICTLY FRIENDS?
A RED FOX BOOK 978 1 849 41206 3

First published in Great Britain by Red Fox Books,
an imprint of Random House Children's Books,
A Random House Group Company

This edition published 2010

1 3 5 7 9 10 8 6 4 2

The Random House Group Limited supports the Forest Stewardship Council
(FSC), the leading international forest certification organization. All our titles that
are printed on Greenpeace-approved FSC-certified paper carry the FSC logo. Our
paper procurement policy can be found at: www.randomhouse.co.uk/paper.htm

Mixed Sources
Product group from well-managed
forests and other controlled sources
www.fsc.org Cert no. TT-COC-2139
© 1996 Forest Stewardship Council
FSC

Red Fox Books are published by Random House Children's Books,
61–63 Uxbridge Road, London W5 5SA

www.**kids**at**randomhouse**.co.uk
www.**rbooks**.co.uk

Addresses for companies within The Random House Group Limited
can be found at: www.randomhouse.co.uk/offices.htm

THE RANDOM HOUSE GROUP Limited Reg. No. 954009

A CIP catalogue record for this book is available from the British Library.

Printed and bound in Great Britain by
CPI Bookmarque, Croydon, CR0 4TD

For Ruth Knowles, 100% sweetheart

Strictly
Friends?

Chapter 1

new home!

from: jakewaltzman@yahoo.com
to: meggyhirstywirsty@gmail.com
sent: 7 September
subject: new home!

Welcome to your new house! Is this the first email
you've got since you arrived? How long has it taken
you to get connected? Has Owen eaten the wiring?
Has everything arrived in one piece?
Can you tell how bored I am??
Missing you already!

from: Megan
to: Jake
sent: 8 September
subject: re: new home!

1

Helloooo! You are so hilarious, how can you be missing
me already? We only said goodbye two days ago!
(Actually, I am kind of missing you a bit. All right, a lot.
But shhhh. I'm supposed to be all happy happy happy
in our lovely new house.)

Sorry I couldn't reply before, I had to go to SCHOOL
today, can you believe it? The day after we move in
and I have to start at a new school! How unfair! But
Mum said it's better to start properly on the first day of
term. Huh. She wasn't the one who had to walk into a
class where EVERYONE else knew each other, wearing
a shiny new uniform that just screams NEWBIE.
Actually, I wasn't the only new person. There's another
girl called Suki who's just moved here too. She and
I sort of clung to each other during the day. Neither
of us understood a word anyone said and we got lost
twice – once on the way to art and once trying to find
the canteen. By the time we got there, they'd run
out of chips! Unbelievable. How can a school with a
thousand pupils run out of chips?!

Anyway, I suppose it was OK for a first day. Everyone
was very nice, and Suki does ballet so we had
something to talk about. She told me about pointe
shoes and I told her about fleckles and other ballroom

steps. Lucky that the other new girl also likes dancing! She's going to this posh ballet school at the weekends. I haven't got a clue where I'm going to go for ballroom lessons, but hopefully there'll be something nearby. Moving seems to have happened so quickly I haven't got my head around it yet – it's almost like I thought it wouldn't really happen. And now we're here!

Anyway. So school was OK but (and don't tell ANYONE I told you this) I kept thinking about Milton Park and everyone there – especially you of course – and although I tried to look really confident, I was shaking inside. I really miss my old school. (I never thought I'd say that about Milton Park, LOL!)

How did your first day back go? Have they re-painted the first-floor classrooms like they said? What are the new people in my old house like? Actually, don't tell me. I'm not sure I can bear it.

I miss you so much! And Milton, and my old house, and the scary snicket where we once met that huge dog, and the post office, and Mrs Connelly at the Spar.

Ahem. The new house is really nice. My bedroom is about twice as big as my old one, and we have a living

room AND a dining room!! Mum is already talking
about having dinner parties, I can't think why. It's not
like we know anyone here yet!

Gotta go, got a gazillion things to unpack. No idea if
everything has made it here in one piece. Dad says
there are six boxes missing but I don't know how he
knows that.

Will write more soon, promise.
Megan xxx

from: Jake
to: Megan
sent: 8 September
subject: re: new home!

I rang you but it went to voicemail. Have you got your
phone switched off? Or were you talking to (gulp)
someone else? How dare you be talking to someone
else when I'm trying to ring!

You'll have to tell me more than that. New school,
new house, yawn, yawn. Suki does ballet? That's kind
of cool. But come on, I want more details! Was Owen

sick on the 200-mile journey from Yorkshire to your soft southern county? How many times did your dad swear at other drivers? Is the new garden as big as it looked in the photos?

Come on, come on! Anyone would think you'd got a lot to do or something!

from: Megan
to: Jake
sent: 10 September
subject: answers at last

What are you like! LOL. I really am sorry, there's just been no time to do anything. Mum and Dad keep sending me from one corner of the house to the other with boxes or random 'stuff'. But they've crashed out in front of the telly now, and Owen is in bed (finally – he's not liking this whole new house thing AT ALL) so I should be able to write a bit more. I rang you back, by the way, but this time YOUR phone went to voicemail. Did you get my message?

So, to answer your questions:

       1.   No, yours wasn't the first email I received.

I got one from DanceWear International, offering me 10% off Capezio shoes. Hah.

2.   It took us nearly 24 hours to get connected, but that was only because Mum had put the modem in her bedside drawer, thinking it was something to do with her hair straighteners.

3.   I still don't know if everything has arrived in one piece. There are twenty-nine boxes left to unpack. I counted them this evening.

4.   Yes, Owen was sick on the journey – twice! How did you guess? It was totally disgusting.

5.   Dad swore at the other drivers forty-one times. (I made that up. I didn't really count. And some of the time I was asleep.)

6.   Yes, the new garden is easily as big as it looked in the photos – in fact, there's a bit that goes round the side of the house too and you can play tennis against the garage wall. Not that I have any idea where my tennis racquet is (is that the right spelling? It looks weird).

The house is lovely, and as I said before, my room is really big. Mum says I can decorate it how I like. I know what you're thinking – multicoloured walls like the last room! But no, I think I might go for turquoise. Or lilac.

I haven't decided yet. Owen wants a huge jungle over his walls, but I think he'd change his mind if he really had one. He's scared of *The Lion King*, remember! He threw this massive tantrum when we arrived – it seems Teddy got lost on the way somehow. We looked everywhere, but he's completely gone. Owen went ballistic. It took Mum two hours to get him to sleep that first night – you know he's never gone to sleep without Teddy before. And in a new house too! Poor Owen, he was really upset. But Mum took him into town the next morning and let him choose something, so he cheered up. He's got this huge snow leopard thing, it's practically bigger than he is! He's called it Snowy. How original – not!

Dad is loving his new job at the architecture firm. Mum says it was worth moving all this way to see the smile on his face. Well, it might be for him, but it wasn't for me. There is nothing to DO here. I don't know anyone and I hate not knowing where anything is either – like the nearest supermarket or cinema or – well, anything. Every time I step outside the door, Mum is paranoid I'm going to be kidnapped or something. She keeps going on about Parchester being such a big town and how I mustn't go anywhere on my own. It's like I'm suddenly six again! And she's constantly on at me

about taking my mobile everywhere 'just in case'. Just
in case of WHAT? Nothing can possibly happen to me
while she's superglued to my side!!

I have been dropping subtle hints though about
how I *need* a new mobile phone. She hasn't noticed
yet.

School is still OK, I guess, but I can't get used to the
number of people around. I always thought Milton Park
was a big school, but this one feels like a whole village
on its own. I asked this girl in my class called Kate if
there were other people who did ballroom dancing
in our year. She said she had no idea, she didn't even
know most of them! Can you imagine not knowing
everyone in your year?! But there are six forms in one
year – six! While Milton Park only has three . . . must
stop thinking about it though or I'll get upset.

Speaking of which! Dancing!! I have been asking
around, but it's like no one's ever heard of ballroom
dancing. Or if they have, they just think of *Strictly
Come Dancing*. Someone said to me, 'Oh, I didn't
realize you could actually learn it.' Well, duh! So I don't
know if there'll be anything nearby I can go to. School
doesn't have ANY dance classes, but they're obsessed
with sport. Hockey, tennis, football . . . but no dancing!

I SO miss it! How can I get by without the rumba, the samba, the foxtrot . . . and the waltz, of course ;-) Our best dance!

Oh no, now I'm feeling homesick. Classes with Laney start again next week, don't they? Tell her hi from me. And don't you dare find a better partner than ME! I can't believe you're going to go back to classes and I won't be there. How long have we been dancing together? Is it eight years? Do you remember how we used to climb over the fence between our gardens so we could practise when the sun was out? And how our mums never knew which house we'd be in?

I'm going to stop before I blub all over the keyboard and break it.
Love to everyone, especially your mad mum.
Megan xxx

from: Jake
to: Megan
sent: 11 September
subject: hugs

You sound kind of down. I'm really sorry. I wish there

9

was something I could say. If it's any help, we all miss you loads here. Amanda was asking after you in class yesterday. And Laney said it wouldn't be the same without you arguing with her about choreography! Even my mum says she can't get used to you not being next door and popping round every five minutes.

And I miss you lots of course. Yeah, eight years – something like that. Wow. Wonder how many hours we've spent together? Most of them practising the waltz, I bet! LOL.

Hang in there. It'll get better, I'm sure. You just need to find a dance class and then everything will be fine. You know how dancing makes it all better!

from: Megan
to: Jake
sent: 12 September
subject: re: hugs

I've seen a poster for a new salsa class starting up. It'll probably be full of beginners, but it's the only thing I can find. Do you think I should go?
Megan xxx

♥ ♥ ♥ ♥ ♥ ♥ strictly friends? ♥ ♥ ♥ ♥ ♥ ♥ ♥

from: Jake
to: Megan
sent: 12 September
subject: salsa

YES.

Chapter 2

it's about attitude

'Salsa?' said Megan's mum, Nicola, frowning as she stared at the oven. 'Just salsa, not any other kind of dancing?' She twiddled one of the dials. 'I can't remember how I made this work yesterday.'

'Yes, just salsa,' said Megan. 'But I thought maybe the dance teacher would know of other classes nearby.'

Nicola nodded. 'Good idea. You should go along. What level are they? The dancers, I mean.'

'I think it's a beginner's class.'

Nicola raised her eyebrows. 'You don't want to be doing that, do you? It'll drive you mad. You haven't been a beginner since you were six.' She sighed. 'Maybe I should just twist all the knobs at once and see what happens.'

Megan reached over and flicked a switch on the wall. The oven pinged on. 'You forgot the fuse switch.'

Nicola gave a short laugh. 'I am such an idiot. It's big and red and says "OVEN" on it, how could I miss it?'

Megan shrugged. 'Can I have a new pencil case?'

'What's wrong with the one you have?'

'It's not big enough. I have to take coloured pencils for maths and they won't fit in.'

Her mother frowned. 'Why would you need coloured pencils for maths?'

'I don't know, it's what they told me. Colouring pie charts or something. So can I have one?'

Nicola glanced at her daughter. Like Megan, she had long auburn hair and green eyes, but there were dark circles under her eyes, and her hair hung limply. She sighed. 'All right. We'll go choose one after school, shall we?' She rubbed her hand over her face. 'I need an early night.'

A small ball of energy rushed into the room. 'Mummy, Mummy, Snowy fell into the fireplace!' Owen held up his new toy.

'Oh, Owen,' said Nicola, reaching for the leopard and brushing at its fur, 'it's covered in soot. I told you not to play near the fireplace. What happened to the fireguard?'

'It sort of collapsed when Snowy was bouncing

on it,' said Owen. 'Can you make him white again, Mummy?'

'I don't know. Probably. But not now, Owen, hey? I'm trying to make dinner.'

'Macaroni cheese, macaroni cheese!' chanted Owen.

'Yes, hopefully,' said Nicola. She cast a pleading look at Megan. 'Assuming I get a minute to make it, that is. Can you amuse Owen for a bit, love?'

Megan felt annoyed. 'Can't he amuse himself?'

'Not without something getting broken,' said her mother in a sharp tone. 'Please, Megan. Just for ten minutes or so.'

'Oh, all right.' Megan glanced at Owen. 'Come on, tinker.'

'Don't call me tinker.' Owen stuck out his bottom lip. 'I don't like it.'

'Whatever. Let's go and play with your toys.'

'They're all boring.'

'What about your castle?'

'Still in a box.' Owen looked mutinous. 'Still got everything in boxes.'

'Well,' said Megan, 'let's unpack one.'

Nicola pulled a face. 'We've ordered a new carpet for his room, remember. Can't have too much stuff out.'

'I hate this house!' Owen announced, and ran out of the room.

Megan rolled her eyes. 'He's such a baby.'

'Megan . . .'

'All right, all right. I'll go and find him.' Megan stomped off towards the stairs. Behind her, she heard her mother give a frustrated sigh before tipping the macaroni into a dish.

♥

Owen was sitting in the middle of his bedroom floor, glaring at his empty bookcase.

'Hey.' Megan sat down next to him. 'You OK?'

'Stupid house. Stupid place. I want to go home.'

'This is home now,' said Megan.

Owen shook his head. 'No, it isn't.'

Megan bit her lip. 'No, it isn't really. I feel the same way. Nothing's in the right place.'

'And everything smells funny.'

'But we have to get used to it,' Megan told him. 'I'm sure we'll be very happy here.'

Owen glanced at her shrewdly. 'You're just saying that.'

'No, I'm not,' Megan lied. There was a bang downstairs. Megan was relieved at the distraction. 'That's the front door. Daddy's home.'

'Hello!' came a voice from the hallway. 'Is this the Hirst residence, or have I arrived at a storage facility?'

'Daddy!' yelled Owen, jumping to his feet and running down the stairs.

'Don't run!' came Nicola's shout.

Megan stood up slowly. She knew exactly how Owen felt. Everything was wrong here. Back home, she knew where everything was – every squeaky stair, every door that needed a special nudge to close properly, every crack in her bedroom ceiling. Here it was all strange, like they shouldn't really be here. It was like going to stay in a holiday cottage – only this wasn't a holiday, it was for the rest of their lives. Well, the foreseeable future anyway.

From downstairs, Megan could hear the voices of her parents floating up to her, punctuated by Owen's questions and comments. Owen would have forgotten their old house within a couple of months, she was sure. But *she* wouldn't. It wasn't just the house itself, it was all those memories. She'd grown up in Milton; it was the only place she'd ever lived. She knew who she was in Milton. Megan from Milton did ballroom dance, played tricks on her next-door-best-friend and splashed in the paddling pool with her little brother.

But here, Megan felt itchy on the inside, like there was something crawling under her skin, making her grumpy and upset.

She had to start all over again, make new friends, find her place. And she wasn't even sure she was going to be the same person she had been back home.

Who was Megan from Parchester?

♥

Megan felt nervous as she waited outside the Alexander Arts Centre. Her mother had walked her round the corner, but Megan had persuaded her not to hang about. 'It'll be starting in a minute,' she said. 'You don't have to wait with me.'

'You're a big girl now,' said Nicola with a grin. 'All right. But I'll come and meet you at the end, OK? At least . . .' Her brow creased. 'Hmm, that could be a bit tricky. It'll be Owen's bedtime. And your dad's working late tonight on some design project.'

Owen, who was trying to balance Snowy on top of a low wall, frowned. 'It's not bedtime for ages and ages yet.'

'Mum, it's only round the corner,' said Megan. 'It takes three minutes. I can walk home on my own after the class.'

'Are you dancing?' asked Owen. He looked around. 'Where's Jake?'

'Jake doesn't dance here,' Megan told him. 'Remember? Jake's back home in Milton.' She swallowed. Going to a dance class without Jake felt like going to school without her left leg.

'I like Jake,' said Owen firmly. 'He makes good Lego models.'

'I don't want you walking home on your own,' said Nicola. 'It'll be late.'

'Seven o'clock is not late, Mum.'

'It'll be dark.'

'No, it won't! It's September, Mum, not the middle of winter!' Megan tried to sound reassuring. 'I'll be fine, honestly.'

Nicola bit her lip in indecision. 'You'll have to walk past that skate park, that's all. It's full of . . . of . . . young people.'

Megan couldn't help but laugh at that. 'Now you're just being silly.'

'Am I?' Her mother looked anxious. 'Maybe I am a bit. All right. You walk home on your own, OK? But keep your head down as you go past the park. Don't make eye contact with people, in case they see you as a target. For mobile phone mugging or something.'

'Mum . . .' Megan rolled her eyes.

'And if you're any later than five past seven, I'm coming out to look for you. With Owen in his pyjamas if necessary.'

Owen giggled. 'You can't go out in your pyjamas. They're not proper clothes.'

Megan felt relieved when her mother had gone. It was hard enough starting again in a new place without your mother cramping your style! She took a deep breath and pushed open the main double doors. The poster had said the salsa class would be in Studio Two. Megan hesitated for a moment and then headed down the corridor in the direction of the sign.

There were several other girls in the corridor already but none of them looked as nervous as Megan felt. They all seemed to know at least one other person, and Megan shrank back against the wall as the little groups arrived and stood around chatting and laughing. There were a couple she thought she recognized from her new school, but she couldn't bring herself to talk to them. Again, she felt a wave of homesickness for Laney's class, where she knew everyone and there was a comforting smell of floor polish and leotards. The corridor here smelled of socks and paint. In the hope that it would make her look more confident, Megan busied herself with changing into her dance shoes. Thankfully, she didn't have to wait long because a young woman covered in coloured scarves and clanking bangles swept into the corridor and said, 'Goodness, isn't it cold! We'd better get started and warm up!'

The studio was a large room with a piano in one corner and not much else. Megan had been secretly hoping for a sprung floor or at least a wall of mirrors, but there was nothing like that here. She felt her heart sink in disappointment. This was nothing like the studio she was used to back home. Clearly this dance class was going to be no use at all to her. She wondered if she could slip out the back without anyone seeing.

'Hello, everyone!' said the young woman in a loud voice. She waved her arms to stop the girls chattering. 'For those of you who don't know me, I'm Corinne, and I teach ballet and tap here at the weekend.' Her eyes swept over the group. 'I must say, I'm really pleased so many of you have come this evening. I know one or two of you, but it's great to see so many new faces.' She caught sight of Megan edging her way to the door. 'Do come in properly,' she called, and waved Megan over. Megan flushed. There was no chance of escaping now!

'I need to say straight away that I'm not ballroom trained,' said Corinne, smiling at Megan, who now felt even less enthusiastic. Not ballroom trained! She'd probably find that she knew more than the teacher! 'But I have done a few classes in my time, and I know there was some interest in starting a group like this. Have any of you done salsa before?'

Megan and another girl put their hands up. 'Excellent,' said Corinne. 'Well, I hope you won't mind too much if we start with the basics.'

There was a sudden clattering outside, and a girl's voice could be heard saying, 'Look, Mum, I've already told you. One class only. I don't *do* dancing. Yes. All right. Look, just go, will you?'

The door burst open and in came a rather dishevelled-looking girl with thick blonde hair scooped into an untidy ponytail. She looked around. 'Really sorry I'm late. It – er – my mum . . . well never mind.' She dumped her jacket and bag on the floor and made an exclamation of annoyance. 'Oh no! Sorry, I seem to have walked half the field in on my shoes.' There was indeed a trail of muddy footprints leading from the door. 'I'll take them off,' said the girl, wrestling with her trainers without undoing the laces.

Megan wanted to laugh. The girl seemed completely oblivious to the fact she'd just interrupted everything. Some of the others were glaring at her, but Megan had to hide her smile. The blonde girl looked up and caught Megan's eye. She grinned back. 'Nearly done.'

Corinne was looking amused too. 'When you've quite finished . . .' She frowned for a moment. 'Don't I know you?'

The girl nodded. 'From *Romeo and Juliet*. I was the Nurse.'

'Ah, that's right,' said Corinne. 'Mari, isn't it? Talked through most of those rehearsals too, didn't you?'

'Not *all* of them,' said Mari, grinning.

'Right,' said Corinne. 'Shall we get started?'

Mari came to stand by Megan. 'I see you brought the right shoes,' she said, glancing at Megan's silver ballroom shoes. 'I'm just going to have to dance in socks.'

'That's all right,' said Megan. 'It won't matter.'

Corinne began explaining the basic salsa step, and Megan looked around the room. There were about twelve of them, she guessed, and all girls of course. She had hardly been expecting anything else, but she felt a bit disappointed nonetheless. This wouldn't be a good class for her. She was way beyond the basics, and she needed a partner to dance with if she wanted to carry on training. Megan wondered just how far away she would need to travel to find one.

To her left, Mari was stomping around in an attempt to follow Corinne. 'This is ridiculous,' she muttered. 'I've got no sense of rhythm.'

Megan laughed. 'I'm guessing it wasn't your idea to come tonight?'

'You're so right,' said Mari with feeling. 'My mum thinks I need to lose some weight. She drew up a long list of things she wanted me to join, but I put my foot down. I mean – *hockey* club?' She shuddered. 'I tried badminton last term but I have no hand–eye coordination and I was just rubbish. This was the only other activity on the list that took place indoors.'

Megan grinned. 'Is that why you said you were only coming for one lesson?'

The expression on Mari's face was comical. 'You heard that? Oh no, how embarrassing. I don't want Corinne to think I've come along to mess about.' She tried the step again. 'My legs just won't do that.'

'Here.' Megan took up position beside her. 'It's quite simple really. Step forward-back-close. Then back-forward-close. That's it.'

'That's it?' Mari looked surprised. 'Doesn't seem like much.'

'It isn't, but the whole dance is based on that basic step.' Megan demonstrated. 'And it's all about timing. One, two three . . . five, six, seven. Like this.'

'Wow,' said Mari. 'You look like you've done it before.'

'I have,' admitted Megan. 'I've been ballroom dancing since I was six.'

'Six!' exclaimed Mari. 'The only thing I've been doing since I was six is eating.' She pulled a face. 'As my mother keeps pointing out.'

Megan hesitated. 'You don't look fat to me.'

'You're sweet. I don't look fat to me either, but Mum keeps trying to feed me brown rice and steamed fish.' She shuddered. 'Grim.'

'OK!' called Corinne. 'Everyone got that step now? Good. The salsa isn't just about the steps though. It's about attitude. You've got to swing your hips . . .'

Megan enjoyed the rest of the class, mostly because of Mari, who made her laugh. There were other girls in the class who were quick to pick up the steps, and it was clear many of them had done some kind of dance before. At least they hadn't spent the whole hour just doing the basic step over and over again, reflected Megan as she changed her shoes. They had learned enough for Corinne to put together a simple routine.

'Please say you'll be my partner again next week,' Mari begged as she pulled on her outdoor shoes. 'I might stand a chance of remembering it then.'

'I thought you weren't coming back next week,' said Megan, amused. 'You said you'd only come for one lesson.'

Mari went slightly pink. 'Well, it wasn't as bad as I thought,' she said. 'I did think maybe the class would be full of stuck-up ballerinas.'

Megan let out a snort of laughter. 'Don't say that too loudly. Nothing wrong with ballet.'

'Indeed not,' said Corinne, who had overheard this. 'Ballet gives you grace and strength, Mari.' She looked at her pointedly. 'Maybe it would be good for you.'

'I am *not* doing ballet,' said Mari emphatically. Her expression softened. 'But this was OK. I think I could do this.'

Corinne turned to Megan. 'I know you've done salsa before. Have you been to ballroom lessons somewhere else?'

Megan nodded. 'We only just moved to the area last week. I'm from Yorkshire. I started ballroom when I was six.'

Corinne looked sympathetic. 'This class will probably be a bit frustrating for you.'

'I was hoping you'd know if there were other classes I could go to,' said Megan hesitantly.

Corinne looked thoughtful, but then she shook her head. 'Not that I can think of. This isn't a very dance-orientated town, as you may have guessed. I mean, there's ballet and tap and jazz. But not ballroom. It's still a bit of a speciality.'

'That's what I thought,' said Megan, though her heart sank. 'Never mind. I quite enjoyed this evening.'

Corinne saw her downcast expression. 'Maybe there's something we can do to use your skills a bit more,' she suggested. 'Leave it with me. I'll think of something.'

The other girls were heading off. Mari looked at Megan. 'So, are *you* coming next week then?'

Megan bit her lip. 'I don't know. I mean, I don't want to be funny, but this class is way too easy for me.'

Mari put on a pleading expression. 'Oh, please come back. I only understood what to do because you were explaining it to me.' She fluttered her eyelashes. 'I'll try not to talk you into the ground if you come again.'

Megan laughed, though she was flattered by what Mari said. 'Well, maybe. If it's the only class around, I guess it's better than nothing.' She glanced up and noticed the clock. It was ten past seven already! 'Oh no! I should be home by now! My mum will be sending out a search party.' She grabbed her bag hastily. 'Thanks, Corinne. See you, Mari.'

'You'd better!' Mari called after her.

It was still light outside, but Megan knew her mother would be anxiously standing by the window, waiting for her to come home. And after she'd promised to be back by five past seven, too! She hoped Mum wouldn't be bundling Owen's coat over his pyjamas as she promised. Megan raced round the corner to the skate park.

'Oof!'

'Oh, God – I'm so sorry!' Megan looked down at the boy lying on the ground. 'I completely didn't see you! Here . . .' She offered him a hand, but the boy pulled himself up, panting.

'Are you blind?' he exclaimed, brushing down his jeans.

Megan felt embarrassed. 'No. I'm sorry, I was in a hurry. Are you all right?'

The boy stared at her. He was taller than Megan, with jet-black hair that looked like it might be dyed. His eyes were a clear pale grey, and his face – well. Megan gulped. He was quite possibly the most good-looking boy she had ever seen, with high, defined cheekbones and dark eyelashes and eyebrows. He looked like a model. 'Who are you?' the boy demanded. 'Are you new here?'

'Yes,' said Megan, but her voice was croaky and

she had to clear her throat. 'Yes,' she said again. 'Just moved in round the corner.'

The boy looked at her searchingly, taking in her shoulder-length auburn hair, her green eyes and her slim figure. He nodded slowly, and a strange expression crossed his face. He seemed about to say something but then changed his mind. Instead, he nodded once more, and said, 'Well, see you.' Then he reached down for a skateboard that until now Megan hadn't even noticed. With a swift movement, the boy stepped onto it and pushed off. They were at the top of a slight slope, and the board quickly picked up speed. Megan watched as he skimmed over a ramp and up another slope. There were a couple of others watching too, but Megan only had time to notice they were two girls and a boy before a voice behind her made her jump.

'Megan! Thank goodness! What are you *doing*?'

Megan turned to see Nicola hurrying over, clutching Owen, who was wearing his pyjamas and protesting loudly.

'Mum! I'm so sorry, it's only ten past, isn't it?'

'Fifteen minutes past,' said Nicola in an acid tone. 'And now I find out you've been standing around chatting.'

'I haven't, honestly.' Megan followed her mother

home, trying to explain about crashing into the boy and having to stop to apologize.

'Well,' said Nicola, as they arrived at the front door, 'one thing's for certain. You won't be walking home alone again.' She turned away from Megan and took Owen straight upstairs, leaving Megan open-mouthed in the hall.

Megan felt angry. OK, so she should have made sure she was out of there a bit faster, but honestly! Talk about over-reacting!

Megan threw her bag on the sofa and sat down in a huff. If she wasn't going to be allowed to walk home on her own, how on earth would she ever get to talk to that boy again? Because she suddenly realized she really, really wanted to.

Chapter 3

have you got a boyfriend yet?

'That's a bit weird.' Jake's voice came loud and clear over the phone. 'Are you sure that's actually what she said?'

'Yes,' said Megan, still in a mood. 'And now she keeps making little digs about how untrustworthy I am. It's ridiculous. Even Dad's told her she's being silly.'

'What did she say to that?'

Megan snorted. 'She went way over the top. Yelled at him about how his new job didn't mean he could get away with no responsibilities at home, or something.'

'Whoa!'

'I know. It was like she totally flipped.'

Jake was silent for a moment. 'Is she OK? I mean, your mum's normally really cool about stuff like this. Why's she off the scale suddenly?'

'I don't know.' Megan picked at a stray thread on

her pillow case. 'I guess maybe she's all worked up over this move. She seems really stressed at the moment. It is a bit awkward, I suppose. We had carpets delivered yesterday and one of them was the wrong colour or the wrong size or something and the carpet people said it was our fault and Mum just hit the roof.'

'Mmm. I guess if your dad is out all day then she's the one who has to sort everything out.' Jake paused a moment and then said, 'Maybe you need to cut her a bit of slack.'

'What do you mean?'

'Don't jump down my throat! I just mean maybe she's taking it out on you because she's got too much to do.'

'Well, that's not fair.'

'I know, Meg. But it's not all about you.' Jake sounded as though he was grinning. 'You're just the nearest person in the firing line.'

Megan scowled. 'Then she should shoot something that doesn't care. Doesn't have feelings.'

'How was the salsa anyway?' asked Jake, hastily changing the subject.

'All right. Too easy.'

'You going back?'

'I don't know.' Megan rolled over and stared at her

bedroom ceiling. 'I sort of said I would, but only because there's nowhere else to go. If I find a better class, then of course I'd ditch the salsa.'

'We missed you at Laney's.' Jake sounded wistful. 'It wasn't the same. And Laney said I'd have to choose a new partner, but I didn't want to.'

Megan swallowed. 'I don't want you to either. I hate the idea of you dancing with someone else.'

'Me too. But I guess I have to.'

'It's all so unfair!' burst out Megan. 'Why did Dad have to go and get a job miles away from home? No one asked me what *I* wanted!'

Jake was silent.

'And I am *trying* to be nice about it all,' Megan went on. 'But it's so hard. Even Suki is starting to get on my nerves.'

'The girl at school?'

'Yeah, the one who does ballet. I've only known her for about five days but already she's starting to annoy me.'

'How?'

'Oh, I don't know. Everything's about her all the time. And she never stops talking about ballet. It's like nothing else exists.' She sighed. 'It's not exactly *what* she says, it's the *way* she says it. I can't explain.'

'If she's that bad, can't you find another friend?'

Megan rolled her eyes, even though she knew Jake couldn't see her. 'You have *no* idea how girls work. You can't just swap friends around like – like clothes.'

'Why not?'

Megan sighed. 'It's too complicated to explain. You wouldn't understand.' She ran her hand through her hair. 'I'm sorry. I'm being all ego-ish. How are things with you?'

She could almost hear Jake shrug. 'All right. New people have moved in next door. They're OK.'

'Oh. What about school?'

'School's OK.'

Megan closed her eyes. Talking to Jake on the phone was nothing like as good as talking to him face-to-face. There was something about the phone that made people go all non-committal and Megan found she'd run out of things to say. And yet she knew that if Jake was actually sitting in her room they'd hardly be able to *stop* talking! There was a long pause. 'So . . .' she said, hoping to find something to fill it.

'Yeah . . .' said Jake.

'Mum and Dad say hi,' said Megan desperately.

'Yeah, mine too.'

'I better go. Got stuff to do.'

'Yeah, me too.'

'OK. Well, talk to you soon.'

'Yeah, sure. And listen, don't give your mum too much of a hard time. If she's being this mad then there must be something wrong.'

'Yeah, you're probably right.'

'See you, then.'

'Bye.'

Megan hung up and stared at the ceiling for a while longer. Talking to Jake on the phone was good and bad – good because it was just so brilliant to hear his voice. Bad because it wasn't the same as being properly together and also because it made her feel even more homesick.

'Megan! You got a minute to help me unpack this?' her mother called up to her.

Megan sighed and rolled off the bed. 'Yeah, down in a sec!' She grabbed a brush and pulled it through her hair, thinking about what Jake had said. It made a lot of sense. Maybe her mum was more stressed by the house move than Megan had thought. Maybe if she was extra-nice and helpful for a bit, Nicola would change her mind about letting Megan out on her own.

That way, Megan had a chance of seeing the boy

in the skate park again. She stared at her reflection in sudden realization.

She had completely forgotten to tell Jake about him!

♥

The bell rang and students poured out of the double doors at the front of the school. Megan found herself jostled and shoved along with the crowd. She wished she'd hung back at the lockers in order to miss the rush, but it was too late now. 'What did you say?' she called to Suki.

Suki turned to shout in annoyance at a boy who had just knocked her bag off her shoulder. She deftly side-stepped another boy and beckoned Megan away from the main doors. 'Giant clods,' she said irritably. 'The boys at my last school were so much more mature.'

'What were you saying as we came out?'

Suki smoothed her hair back into her ponytail. 'I said there's a ballet workshop coming up after Christmas. With the Ballet Formidable.'

'Oh yes?'

Suki's jaw dropped. 'Don't you know who they are?'

'Umm . . .'

'They did that new interpretation of *Sleeping Beauty*. The one with two women playing the leads? People are saying they're the new Adventures in Motion Pictures.'

'Oh right.' Megan pretended she knew what Suki was talking about. 'Yeah, of course – I'd forgotten.'

'They're holding a dance workshop. It's not for months yet, but places are already getting booked up. My ballet teacher's getting a place for me, do you want me to ask for one for you too?'

Megan flushed. 'Oh, that's very kind of you, but ballet's not really my thing.'

Suki looked puzzled. 'But you've had ballet lessons as well as ballroom, haven't you?'

'N-no.'

'Oh!' Suki was taken aback. 'Oh, I see. Sorry,' she added hastily. 'I thought you were serious about a career in dance, that's all.'

Megan felt annoyed. 'What's that got to do with anything?'

'It's just that my teacher says anyone who dances, whatever the dance style, should have a strong grounding in ballet. It helps with practically every other style there is. Strength and grace and all that.'

'Well, I don't know if I'm actually going to dance

professionally,' said Megan, uncomfortable. 'I just like doing it at the moment.'

Briefly, Suki's chin tilted up and she seemed to be regarding Megan down the length of her slightly pointed nose. Then she smiled in a patronizing way. 'Of course. Sorry. I forget that not everyone is as ambitious as me. It's lovely that you enjoy dancing as a hobby.'

Megan tried to ignore the feeling that she was being patronized. 'So you're going to this workshop then?'

Suki nodded. 'I can't wait. They sometimes look out for potential members of the company too!'

'Wow. That would be brilliant.' A thought struck Megan. 'How come you didn't go to a ballet school, Suki? I mean, if you're that good, shouldn't you be somewhere they do dance in school? Parchester Grammar isn't exactly . . .' She stopped. Suki's face had flamed red. 'Sorry. Did I say something wrong?'

Suki shook her head violently. 'No, no, it's fine. I did try to get into the Royal Ballet School, if you must know. But they said my feet were the wrong shape.'

Megan stared. 'Your feet?'

'It's very important,' said Suki, her voice high and strained, 'to have the right shaped feet for pointe work.'

'Oh, I see.'

'Of course, ballroom isn't so strict,' said Suki. 'You can be practically any shape to do that.'

Megan opened her mouth to reply, but Suki had pulled out her mobile and was punching buttons. 'See you tomorrow, Megan. I've got to get something sorted out.' She put the phone to her ear, flicked a quick smile at Megan and then walked away.

Megan stared after her. Suki had this way of saying things that really got up her nose. And the funny thing was, Suki didn't have a clue she was doing it. She probably thought she was being really nice to Megan!

A tall boy with spots bumped hard into Megan, nearly knocking her over. 'Hey!' she said, but he just glanced back at her and grunted. What was wrong with everyone here? Didn't anyone have manners?

Megan stomped out of the school gates, scrabbling for her own mobile. She would text Jake. He would know what to say to cheer her up. She started typing:

Having day from HELL here evry1 so rude and
boring. Miss u!

'Megan!' It was her mum, holding firmly onto Owen's hand and waving at her. 'Over here.'

Megan took a deep breath. She was trying to be extra nice to Nicola at the moment, after the conversation with Jake. Stapling a smile to her face, she headed over. 'Hi! You OK?'

'We're fine.' Nicola smiled. 'Owen made you some fairy cakes.' She looked pointedly at Megan, as if to say, *Be very grateful*.

Owen thrust out a bag of unidentifiable mush. 'They're special.'

Megan looked down. 'They certainly are. Uh – thank you.'

'I made them *all* myself,' Owen told her proudly.

Behind him, Nicola mouthed, 'Don't eat them', and Megan nodded in understanding.

'Have you got a boyfriend yet?'

'What?' asked Megan, startled.

'Have you got a boyfriend?' persisted Owen. 'Jessica at playgroup asked me if I could be her boyfriend. She said everyone has one. Have *you*?'

'Um . . . not exactly.'

'Why not? Doesn't anyone want to be yours?'

'Owen,' Nicola interrupted, 'have you seen that big blue car over there? I think it's a Jaguar.'

Owen's gaze swivelled in excitement. Then he drooped. 'You are so silly, Mummy. That's not a Jaguar. Don't you know anything about cars?'

'No,' said Nicola humbly. 'Not really, Owen. I have to rely on you to tell me.' She and Megan exchanged looks.

'Thanks,' said Megan.

'No problem.' They started off down the road.

'Jaguars,' Owen went on, 'have a jaguar on the front of the bonnet. Like a little statue. Unless it's been nicked.'

'Nicked?' Nicola raised her eyebrows. 'Where did you hear that word?'

'Daddy,' responded Owen cheerfully. 'He said sometimes cars get nicked. And phones. And – other stuff.'

'Mum,' said Megan, wondering if now was a good time, 'do you think sometimes I could walk home from school on my own? It's not far, after all.'

Nicola looked around with a worried expression. 'There are so many kids at this school. I'm concerned that we don't really know anyone yet.'

'I know. But this isn't Milton, Mum. I'm not *going* to get to know everyone here. That's just how it is.' Megan composed herself again. 'Mum, I'm not a child any more. And I had loads more freedom in Milton. I know this isn't the same, but I'm old enough to be trusted, aren't I?'

'Well . . .'

'And I've got my phone with me all the time.' Megan waved it at her just as it beeped to say there was a text.

'I suppose so,' said Nicola, momentarily distracted by Owen stopping to pick up an empty sweet wrapper. 'Put that back, Owen, it's dirty.'

'But if I throw it on the pavement now, Mummy, isn't that being naughty? I mean, I should put it in the bin, shouldn't I?'

Megan pressed home her advantage. 'Other kids my age don't get picked up by their parents at the school gate. It'd be easier for me to fit in at my new school if I didn't stick out like a sore thumb.'

'What have you done to your thumb?' asked Owen, interested.

'Nothing. It's just a saying.'

'Oh.' Owen ran to the nearest bin and carefully deposited his sweet wrapper.

'Mum?'

'All right.' Nicola caved in. 'Tomorrow you can walk back on your own, OK?'

'Thanks.'

'I do appreciate this is difficult for you, Megan. I just don't want you to take any unnecessary risks while we don't really know the area.'

'I know, Mum. And I won't do anything stupid.'

Megan took a quick glance at her phone. The text was from Jake:

> UR in hell? Saw Laney in town and she said I have 2 dance with COLLEEN 2nite! AAARGH!

Megan smiled in spite of herself. Colleen Quirk was a very enthusiastic member of their dance class – almost too enthusiastic. Give her a twirl to do and she would practically fling herself into outer space. She had no control at all, though she was always saying, 'Tell me how to get better. I want to be good!' Jake had always been quite rude about Colleen behind her back. Megan giggled to herself as she imagined Jake's expression when he heard he would have to dance with her. Then she felt another wave of homesickness – it should be *her* dancing with Jake, not Colleen!

Megan sighed and pocketed her mobile again. Her mother and Owen had already disappeared round the corner, so she hurried to catch up. It was no good getting all sad about Milton. This was her home now and she was just going to have to get used to it. No matter how much she hated the idea.

Chapter 4

Nurse Megan

After the first few days, Nicola agreed that Megan could walk to and from school on her own permanently, and even let her go by herself to the salsa class the following week. Megan spent an extra ten minutes getting ready before setting off, but to her disappointment, the good-looking boy wasn't in the skate park.

'You lost something?' asked Mari, coming up just as Megan reached the arts centre. 'You keep looking around.'

'What? Oh – no. No, nothing.' Megan smiled at Mari. Her hair was escaping from her ponytail again, and she looked as though she'd put her clothes on in the dark. 'You came again then.'

Mari smirked. 'So did you.'

Megan laughed. 'I guess I did.'

'You realize,' said Mari, taking her arm as they went into the building, 'you're my personal salsa coach now, don't you? I can't get through this class without you.'

'Well, then I guess I'd better let you know my hourly rates,' said Megan mock-seriously. 'Hang on, I've got a price list here somewhere.' She rummaged in her bag.

Mari stopped short, staring at her in horror. 'Rates?'

Megan burst out laughing. 'Your face, Mari! I'm kidding!'

Mari clutched her chest dramatically. 'Don't *do* that to me! I nearly had a heart attack!'

Much to her surprise, Megan enjoyed her second class even more than the first. The other girls in the class had quickly found out about her background in ballroom, and Mari wasn't the only one to ask for help whilst Corinne was going over steps and routines. Even Corinne turned to her at one point and said, 'Did I do a right turn here, Megan, or was it back into open position?'

Megan enjoyed helping out. Back in Laney's class, she and Jake had never stood out particularly because all the others were so good too. But here, people were impressed by her knowledge and technique. 'I don't know how you can remember all those steps,' puffed Mari, her face pink from the exertion. 'And how come you're not even breaking a sweat?'

'Practice,' said Megan, grinning. 'Come on, let's do that bit again.'

By the end of the lesson, Corinne had asked Megan if she would take a couple of the girls to practise at one end of the studio whilst Corinne worked with the others. Megan felt a surge of pride that Corinne wanted her to take on such responsibilities.

As they packed up, Mari looked enviously at Megan's shoes. 'I wish I had shoes like those,' she said. 'I'm not a big shoe fan, but those are so pretty. I love the strap over the top and the cute heels. And they're silver too – they look so professional.'

'What size are your feet?' Megan handed them over. 'Try them on – sorry, they're hot, I've been wearing them all through class.'

'Are you sure?' Mari slipped a shoe onto her left foot. 'Perfect fit!'

Megan grinned. 'Tell you what then – why don't you borrow them for a while? I've got about six different pairs of ballroom shoes – I don't know where they all are at the moment because everything's still in boxes – but you're welcome to those until you get some of your own.'

'Wow – really?' Mari stared at her for a second and

then suddenly gave her a hug. 'That's so kind, you are sweet. Thank you so much. You know, you remind me of my friend Fliss.'

'Yeah?'

'She's really sweet and helpful too. A good friend.'

'You should bring her along to salsa,' Megan told her.

'I *so* would,' replied Mari as they headed out of the studio, 'but she's on location at the moment.'

Megan stared. 'She's what?'

'On location. You know – filming. She's in a TV series.'

Megan stared. 'Wow! That's amazing. How did that happen?'

'Well . . .' Mari took a breath. 'We did this play over the summer. *Romeo and Juliet*. And Fliss was playing Juliet and she was just totally brilliant. And this TV producer came along to watch and he really liked her, and so he asked her along to an audition for his new show.'

'It sounds like something out of a dream,' said Megan.

'It was! And she got the part and she started filming about a week ago and she's having to miss school and everything!'

Corinne came out of the main building to find

them still standing chatting. 'Haven't you got homes to go to?' she asked, amused.

'Mari was just telling me about her friend who's on TV,' said Megan.

'Ah yes,' said Corinne. 'Fliss. A very talented girl.' She pulled the main doors shut behind her. 'A classic case of being in the right place at the right time. Even though it almost didn't happen.' She nodded to the girls. 'See you next week. And thanks for all your help, Megan.'

'What did she mean?' asked Megan, as Corinne headed off, her bracelets jangling loudly.

'Fliss got injured,' said Mari. Her face darkened. 'Just before the dress rehearsal. She fell off the balcony ladder.'

'That's terrible.'

'And it wasn't an accident. This evil girl put oil on the ladder deliberately so that Fliss would fall off.'

Megan's jaw dropped. 'But that's— Why?'

'She wanted Fliss's part,' said Mari, shrugging. 'But she was rubbish. Completely over the top. She did the dress rehearsal and it was like the worst acting you'd ever seen. Victoria and I nearly walked out.'

'Victoria?'

'My other friend.'

'Oh, right. So what happened?' Megan knew she should be getting home, but this story was the most exciting thing she'd heard since arriving in Parchester. And it was so easy to talk to Mari! She felt like she'd known her for ages, even though this was only the second time they'd met.

'Fliss came back and confronted her,' said Mari with something like pride in her voice. 'And Fliss had oil marks on her shoes, so there was nothing this girl could do. She was completely – what's the word? Convicted? Anyway, we all knew it was her, and she sort of incriminated herself too. So she got thrown out of the show. And good riddance too.'

'But wasn't Fliss injured?'

'She was, but her wrist was only sprained, not broken. And she bumped her head. But she was OK to come back and do the performance. And was *totally* brilliant, I might add.' Mari beamed. 'I always told her she was talented, but she never believed me. And then this TV guy came and put her in his show!'

Megan shook her head in awe. 'That's an amazing story. Like something out of a book.'

'I know. Maybe one day I'll write the story of Fliss's life.' Mari grinned. 'It'd be more interesting than mine.' She sighed. 'Anyway, I'd better go.'

'Me too. You coming next week?'

Mari grinned. 'Are you kidding? This is way better than hockey.'

♥

'She sounds like a laugh,' Jake commented that evening over the phone. 'I can't talk long, Stephen will be back with fish and chips any minute.'

'She is. I really like her. I wish she went to my school.'

'Suki still being annoying?'

Megan screwed up her nose. 'I don't think she means to be. She just has this habit of saying things the wrong way. Even when she's trying to be nice. She basically told me the other day that I couldn't be any good at ballroom if I'd never done ballet.'

'What!' Jake exploded. 'That's ridiculous! The two are *completely* different!'

'I know. And I tried to say that, but she's got this ballet teacher who tells her all this stuff and she believes it.'

'I'd have punched her on the nose,' said Jake firmly.

'No you wouldn't,' said Megan. 'You've never punched anyone.'

49

'All right,' Jake admitted, 'but I'd have wanted to.'

'Well, it doesn't matter. She wasn't trying to be rude. I think she just doesn't think about things before she says them.'

'Really?' Jake's voice took on a quizzical tone. 'That reminds me of someone I know . . . now who could it be?'

Megan laughed. 'I am nowhere near as bad as Suki.'

'Hang on a minute . . .' Jake's voice went quiet for a moment and then he came back on the line. 'Stephen's just come in and Mum says we have to eat now.'

'Oh, OK.' Megan felt disappointed. She felt like there was so much more she needed to tell Jake. 'Talk tomorrow then?'

'Uh, not sure. Think we might be going round to the neighbours'. They've got a welcome drinks thing.'

'What, the ones in my old house?'

'Yeah. I've got to be on my best behaviour.' Jake sounded as though he was grinning. 'Maybe the day after. See you, Meg.'

'Bye.'

Megan hung up and sat back on her bed. She hadn't had a chance to tell Jake about the boy again – the one in the skate park. Even as his face swam into her mind, she felt a sharp twinge of excitement. His eyes – that startling grey – and the strange way he'd looked at her. She felt dizzy just thinking about him. And it wasn't the first time she'd thought about him since the previous week, either . . .

She wondered why he hadn't been there this evening. Where did he live? Which school did he go to? There had been two girls with him, hadn't there? Was one of them his girlfriend?

'Oh, for goodness' sake,' said Megan out loud. 'You don't even *know* him!'

But when she went to bed, she was already figuring out when she could walk past the skate park again.

♥

Now that her mum had said it was all right to go out on her own, Megan found all the excuses she could to walk past the skate park. Fortunately, the post office and the small supermarket were near the arts centre, so there was often a letter to post or a pint of milk to pick up . . .

Much to her excitement, the boy was there most days after school, and Megan began to recognize the people he was with too. There was another boy, shorter and less good-looking. He liked to whoop with excitement as he raced up a ramp on his skateboard. He was kind of stocky, with close-cropped brown hair and slightly sticky-out ears. There was a girl with the sort of long blonde hair Megan had only seen in shampoo adverts before. She seemed to laugh a lot, though Megan was never sure if she was actually amused or laughing for the sake of it. The other girl was very slim with almond-shaped eyes and long dark hair that often fell in her face. She reminded Megan of a girl she had known at Milton Park who was from Thailand. This girl sat and watched the others a lot, especially the tall dark boy.

Megan was fairly sure none of them went to her school. The boys sometimes wore a school tie that she didn't recognize, and she never saw any of them in the corridors at her own school. She was beginning to come to the conclusion that she would never actually get to speak to the tall boy again. She was destined to watch from a distance for ever.

And then one day, all that changed. Megan was walking back from the shops with a packet of raisins and a TV guide. She rounded the corner of the skate park as usual and immediately looked for the tall boy. He wasn't hard to spot. He was lining up his skateboard on what looked like a makeshift ramp, made out of planks of wood, corrugated iron and bricks. It didn't look at all safe, but the boy was cheerfully calling to his friends, 'Three-sixty off the end, right? Get your fiver ready, Paul, you'll have to pay up in a minute!'

The stocky boy called back, 'No way! You can't pull that off. Get *your* money ready.'

The thin dark-eyed girl was anxious. 'Please be careful, Danny,' she begged, whilst the blonde girl just laughed.

'Don't blame me if you break both your legs.'

Megan stopped still, her eyes fixed on Danny. At last she knew his name! He was lining up his board when he glanced over and saw her watching him. There was a flash in his eyes, and then he grinned. Automatically, Megan felt herself smile back. He had such confidence! She had no doubt that whatever he was planning, he could surely do.

Danny paused for a moment, gathering his concentration. Then he kicked off the ground. His board slid down towards the ramp, gaining speed by the inch. By the time it hit the beginning of the ramp, the wind was blowing Danny's hair flat against his head. His face was focused, and his feet shifted tiny amounts to allow for the uneven surface. Megan held her breath. He was going to do it! It just needed a smooth take-off from the end of the ramp, and then he would be flying high with the force of the jump . . .

But just as Danny reached the edge of the ramp, it buckled under his weight, and Megan gasped as the whole piece of corrugated iron slid off the bricks and crashed to the ground, taking Danny and his skate-board with it. There was an almighty crash as boy, board and bricks exploded in a shower of dust and debris.

'Oh my God!' Megan was already rushing down the slope towards him. 'Are you all right?'

Danny was lying on his back amongst a heap of rubbish, groaning.

'Don't try to move,' said Megan breathlessly. 'You might have broken something.'

There was a peculiar noise, and at first Megan thought, to her horror, that Danny was crying. Then she realized he was laughing. Danny sat up and looked at her, his shoulders shaking. 'What a rush!' he said, his eyes flashing. 'Woo-hoo!' He glanced down at his knees and grinned at the scuffing on his trousers. 'There'll be some good grazes under there,' he said confidently.

Megan sat back on her heels and glared at him. 'Aren't you hurt?'

'Nah, not really. I've had worse.'

Megan glanced up. Danny's friends were heading over, exchanging amused looks and trying not to laugh. 'I suppose that explains why your friends don't seem too worried. More fool me. I thought you'd fallen really badly.'

'So you came rushing over to do your nurse bit,' said Danny, grinning. 'That's so cute.'

Megan scowled. 'Well, if you're fine . . .' She started to get up, but Danny grabbed her arm.

'You've been hanging around for the last week,' he said. 'Who are you?'

Megan's jaw dropped. He had noticed her! 'I – uh – I'm Megan.'

'Megan what?'

Megan felt dizzy under his intense stare. His eyes were like the sky on a freezing day. 'Megan Hirst. I'm new here, remember? We met once before.' She nearly bit her tongue – trust her to remind him of the time she'd knocked him down!

He stared at her for a moment, and then his expression relaxed and he let go of her arm. 'Megan Hirst,' he said, as if trying out her name on his tongue. 'Nurse Megan.'

Megan gave a shaky laugh. 'Oh, no. I couldn't be a nurse. Can't stand blood.'

'Really?' His head tilted to one side. 'Then why did you rush over?'

'Oh.' Megan was stumped. She felt a blush creep over her cheeks. 'I don't know. I just – well, I thought you might be hurt.'

'Danny!' The blonde girl had reached them first. 'You absolute doughnut, what did you think you were doing?'

The boy called Paul was sniggering loudly. 'You owe me a fiver.'

Danny scowled. 'The ramp collapsed. I never got a chance to try it.'

'You still owe me.'

The dark-eyed girl was shifting nervously from foot to foot. 'Are you OK? That looked like a really bad one.' Her voice was so soft Megan hardly caught the words, and she pulled at her long black hair anxiously.

'I'm fine,' said Danny.

The blonde girl looked pointedly at Megan. 'Who's this?'

'This is Megan Hirst,' said Danny, with a smirk. 'She's not a nurse.'

Megan felt embarrassed. She didn't belong in this group, and the blonde girl was wearing an expression of disgust. She got to her feet. 'I just came to see if he was all right.' She glanced down at Danny. 'I should be going now.'

'Been doing the shopping?' asked the blonde girl in a sneery voice.

Megan realized she was still clutching the raisins and TV guide. But the girl's tone annoyed her. 'How did you guess?' she retorted.

Danny snorted with laughter. The blonde girl glared. The other girl retreated behind her curtain of hair. Megan thought to herself, *These people are really weird*. 'Well,' she said politely, 'it was nice to meet you.'

'You want a go?' asked Danny, as she turned away.

Megan felt baffled. Who *was* this boy anyway? 'A go?' she repeated.

Danny got to his feet with a grimace. 'On my board. You want a go?'

Megan glanced at the blonde girl. She didn't look very friendly. Neither did the dark-eyed girl. 'Oh, I don't think so . . .'

'Ever been on a skateboard?' asked Danny.

'Er – no, but . . .'

'Right. Here's your chance.' Without waiting for her to reply, Danny fished out his skateboard from the pile of debris, brushed off the gravel and brick dust, and tucked it under his arm. Then he held out his hand. 'Come on. We'll start on the flat.'

Almost hypnotized, Megan took his hand. It was cool and rough in places – from all the grazes, she supposed. *I should be getting home*, said a little voice inside her head. *Why am I still standing here?*

Now Danny was putting the board on the concrete and showing her how to place her feet. 'Put down your stuff,' he said. 'You need both hands free to help you balance.'

Megan did as she was told. The board wobbled under her feet. 'I thought it was fixed,' she said in some surprise. 'I mean, I thought the top bit stayed flat.'

Danny shook his head. 'It's called a deck. It needs to be able to tilt in all directions. It's got suspension, like a car. Try rocking it from side to side.' He watched her critically. 'You've got good balance.'

'I'm a dancer,' said Megan, hoping this would sound impressive, but Danny seemed barely to hear her. His whole attention was focused on her feet.

'Now try pushing it along a bit.'

He was a good teacher. It was only when Megan heard a snort that she looked up and realized the other three had been watching all along. The blonde girl had flung one arm casually over Paul's shoulders and was busy whispering in his ear. The dark-eyed girl perched on the edge of a ramp and glared at Megan through her hair. The heat suddenly rose in Megan's face and she stepped off the board. 'Look,' she said, 'I don't think I'm really wanted here.'

Danny looked around in astonishment. 'What are you talking about?' His expression cleared. 'Oh, you mean the girls? Don't take any notice of them.' Megan thought this was a bit unkind, seeing as they were both within earshot. The Thai-looking girl's lips tightened. Danny laughed. 'They're just jealous because I won't let them have a go on my board.'

'Who'd want to?' the blonde girl flashed back.

Danny grinned. 'That's Samantha. She's my sister, so she has to hate everything I do.'

His sister! Megan automatically felt relieved. Samantha was far more glamorous than she was. But if she was Danny's sister, then at least she wasn't his girlfriend . . . Her gaze swept over to the dark-eyed girl.

'That's Jasmine,' said Danny dismissively. 'She hangs around with us.'

Jasmine drooped slightly at Danny's words, as though disappointed by what he'd said.

'Go on.' Danny's pale gaze fastened on Megan again. 'Have another go. Really.'

Why is he being so nice to me when the others don't want me around? Megan wondered. She felt strangely flattered. Danny had actually noticed her over the past week! And he'd obviously forgiven her for knocking into him. 'How long have you been skateboarding?' she asked, as she stepped back onto the board.

Danny shrugged and looked at Paul. 'Years,' he said.

Paul nodded in agreement. 'I've had six boards altogether.'

'Six!' Megan stared at him. 'Why?'

'Some got broken,' said Danny, with a grin. Paul grinned too, as though it were all a big joke. 'But it's like buying anything. The more you spend, the better the deck. I'm saving up for new Alien Workshop wheels.'

This went completely over Megan's head. 'Just the wheels?'

'Sure,' said Danny. 'You buy everything separately and then build it yourself.'

'You mean it doesn't come like this?' asked Megan, staring down at the black and white graphic design under her feet. 'You have to put it together yourself? Like a – a bookshelf?'

Paul frowned, but Danny laughed. 'Yeah, like a

bookshelf.' He seemed to find this very funny. 'A bookshelf! You can't skate on a bookshelf.'

'Bet you could,' Paul broke in. 'You could slide along the spine.'

Danny swung round, his eyes alight. 'We haven't done a bookshelf before. There's a house down my road that's got a skip outside. Bet they're throwing out a bookshelf.'

Megan looked from one to the other, bewildered. These boys were on another planet! Samantha yawned loudly. 'Are you going to do any more tricks, or are you just going to stand around and chat?' she asked in a bored voice. 'Because we need to go to the club and get it sorted.'

'Yeah,' said Jasmine, who was biting her nails. 'Me too.'

Samantha rolled her eyes. She turned to Megan. 'You going tonight?'

'Going to what?' asked Megan.

'The youth club thing, of course,' said Samantha. 'Didn't you know about it?'

Megan tried to think. 'A poster at the arts centre?' she hazarded. 'Something for charity?'

Samantha nodded and flicked her shiny hair over her shoulder. 'I'm on the committee.'

Megan was surprised. Samantha didn't look like

the sort of girl who'd want to bother herself with committees. 'Oh, right. Sorry, no, don't think I can make it.' If it had been Mari asking, Megan would have been there like a shot. But something about Samantha made her feel uncomfortable. And a whole youth club of people she didn't know . . . Megan wasn't sure she was ready for that!

Samantha shrugged. 'Oh well.'

Megan felt she should try to continue the conversation so that she didn't seem too rude. 'Which charity is it?'

'Childline,' said Samantha.

'Oh, right. That's a good one. I knew a girl who rang Childline once. She said they were really nice.'

'I didn't pick it,' said Samantha.

'Oh.' Megan ran out of things to say. It was funny, she thought briefly, how you just clicked with some people, like Mari, whereas with others . . . it was so much harder.

Danny finished his discussion about the bookshelf with Paul and turned back to Megan. 'You haven't got very far,' he said. 'Just go up and down a bit.'

Megan wobbled from one end of the park to the other and then back again. She wasn't sure she liked the feeling of the board beneath her. It made her slightly sea-sick. But Danny's expression was approving. 'Good,' he said. 'You're doing really well for a beginner.'

Despite herself, Megan flushed. 'Do you think so?' What *was* it about Danny? Why was she so anxious to have his approval?

Danny looked her up and down. Megan felt an absurd desire to cover herself up with something, even though she was fully clothed. 'You've got the right build for boarding,' he said. 'Or BMXing.'

'Huh?'

'Danny is obsessed with wheels,' said Samantha, but she spoke with a kind of pride. 'He can drive anything – go-karts, bikes, cars.'

'*Cars?*' Megan was astonished.

Danny smiled, and his eyes lit up with silver. 'They're the best,' he said enthusiastically. 'Our uncle has a Jeep he lets me drive on his farm. It's awesome.'

Megan's jaw dropped. 'A real *Jeep?*'

'Yeah, a real one.'

Megan stared at him. Danny was full of surprises, she thought. She'd never met anyone like him before. He drove a Jeep? Wasn't that illegal? And dangerous?

'I could take you for a drive sometime,' offered Danny.

'No you couldn't,' said Samantha. 'Uncle Ed would kill you. He won't let *me* come in the car with you.'

'Uncle Ed wouldn't have to know,' said Danny carelessly.

Megan was fascinated. 'You'd take the car without asking him?'

He shrugged. 'Maybe.'

Megan knew she should be appalled by this, but somehow it just added to her awe. Samantha spoiled the moment by commenting acidly, 'He'd beat you to dust if you did.'

Jasmine gave a high giggle and then fell silent in embarrassment.

There was a pause. 'So are you finished then?' asked Samantha.

Danny frowned. 'What?'

Samantha leaned forward to enunciate her words very clearly. 'Have – you – finished – teaching – your – new – pupil? Because you promised you'd help me put up the decorations at the youth club for tonight.'

Danny rolled his eyes. 'We've got all day. There's no hurry, is there?' Jasmine giggled again and Danny shot her an exasperated look. 'Yeah, all right, I'm finished.' He turned to Megan. 'See you tomorrow,' he told her. 'Same time.'

Megan's breath caught in her throat. 'Uh – tomorrow?'

He nodded, and his eyes seemed to glitter in the light. 'Yeah – don't you want another go on the board? I can teach you some tricks.'

'Yeah, if you're sure. Thanks!' Megan was sure her face had flamed bright red, and she knew Jasmine was glaring at her.

Danny nodded, and he and Samantha set off across the park, arguing about something. Paul trailed after them, not even bothering to say goodbye. Jasmine looked uncertainly from the disappearing group to Megan, and then suddenly pulled her hair back from her face. 'He's not what you think,' she said to Megan, and her voice sounded brittle.

'Pardon?'

Jasmine nodded. 'You'll see.' She gave Megan another strange look before hurrying away.

Megan stood still for a moment, her head spinning. She felt like she'd just spent time in an alternative world of some kind. It was almost as though Danny and the others spoke a language she didn't understand. What they said seemed to mean something else entirely . . . Megan rubbed her face briskly. *Snap out of it!* she told herself. *They're just a bit different to what you're used to, that's all. But Danny seemed to like you . . .*

He remembered her from before. He wanted to

teach her how to ride his skateboard. He thought she was interesting . . .

Megan had the oddest feeling her parents wouldn't approve, but she couldn't help smiling all the way home. And she couldn't wait for tomorrow!

Chapter 5

want to see my scars?

Megan stared at the computer screen and deleted the three sentences she'd already written. Why was it so hard to tell Jake about Danny? Jake was her best friend. He knew her better than anyone. He'd understand, wouldn't he? Or *would* he? Megan shook her head in frustration. She'd never had a boyfriend before. Jake hadn't had a girlfriend either. They'd both had crushes on people, but this . . . well, this felt a bit different. How did you talk to your best friend about boys if your best friend *was* a boy?

from: Megan
to: Jake
sent: 26 September
subject: salsa and skateboards

Hey you!
Salsa is going OK – actually, I'm kind of having fun. You

remember I told you about Mari? She was telling me
all about her friend who's in a TV series – how cool is
that! And apparently this friend had a nasty accident in
the summer when she was acting in *Romeo and Juliet*
and fell off the ladder leading to the balcony. Only it
wasn't an accident because this other girl put oil on the
rungs so she'd fall off. Don't you think it sounds like
something out of a book? If it hadn't been Mari telling
me, I'm not sure I'd have believed it. But I don't think
Mari can lie. She just opens her mouth and all
her feelings come spilling out. She's the main reason
I'm still going to salsa, actually. She's got no rhythm at
all but she tries really hard and she's always asking me
for help. You'd think I was the teacher, not Corinne!
In fact, Corinne has even asked me for help in the
classes too!

I've been meaning to tell you. I met this group of
kids skateboarding yesterday. They're really cool, but
they try to do stuff that looks so dangerous! This boy
called Danny started to teach me how to skateboard
but I was a bit rubbish. He said I had good balance
though – I told him it was all these years of dancing!
Maybe it's time I learned a new skill? I'm not sure I like
skateboarding much but then you have to practise to
get good at something, and Danny was really patient

with me. He said he'd meet me today and teach me a
bit more.

How's your mad mum and your stepdad? How did
the drinks thingy go next door? You haven't told me
anything about the new people there! (I know I told
you not to, but now I kind of want to know.)

Mx

Megan sat back. Should she have said more about
Danny? But Jake hated girls who went all 'gaga'
over the boys they fancied. She didn't want to make
it sound like she was going on about Danny all the
time.

She clicked on 'send' before she could change her
mind. It was late Sunday morning, and since she
had met Danny and the others at 11 a.m. yesterday, it
seemed likely that they would be there now.

'You're going where?' asked her mum in some
surprise.

Megan tried not to blush. 'You know I told
you I'd met some kids in the skate park yesterday?'
She saw her mother's expression and hurried on.
'They're really nice, honestly. They showed me
how to skateboard.' Nicola's eyebrows climbed

even higher. 'It was fun,' Megan said defensively.
'They said they'd teach me a bit more today. Can
I go?'

'Well . . .' Nicola hesitated. 'It's Sunday morning . . .'

Megan looked hopefully at her dad. Bryan looked
puzzled. 'Why can't she go out this morning? It's not
as though we're doing anything.'

'I never said she couldn't,' said Nicola. 'I just – I
don't know. Sundays are family time, aren't they?'

Bryan smiled at Megan. 'You go and have fun, love.
You're going to stay in the skate park, right? You're not
going anywhere else?'

'No,' said Megan. 'Just practising in the park.'

'I think it's great you've met some new friends,' said
her dad.

'So do I!' retorted her mum. 'You always make me
sound like the bad cop!'

'Bad cop bang bang!' said Owen gleefully. 'With a
big gun!'

Nicola's attention was immediately diverted. 'I
don't want you talking about big guns,' she told him.
'They're very dangerous.'

Owen nodded. 'I know. Moses at playgroup told
me he saw a man get shot in a film. His head blew up
and went splat.'

'Your friend Moses watches the wrong sorts of films,' said Bryan.

Owen shrugged. 'He said it wasn't as good as *Finding Nemo* anyway.'

'So I'm going out then,' said Megan.

Nicola turned to her. 'Of course you can, love. Just take your phone.'

Megan's heart was pounding as she walked to the skate park. Would he be there? What would she do if he wasn't? She felt strangely itchy all over, as though her skin were tingling on the inside. *This is ridiculous!* she told herself. *You don't even know him! And the others didn't seem that keen to have you around, did they? Why do you even want to see him again?*

But Megan knew the answer to that one. Danny had a magnetic quality; he seemed to draw her into his world. He was wild – and she'd never met anyone like him before.

As she rounded the corner to the park, Megan felt slightly sick with anticipation. But there he was! Grinding the board along a railing! Paul followed a few feet behind, both boys whooping and yelling with excitement.

Megan looked around quickly. At the far end was a children's playground; bright and colourful. She could just make out the figures of Samantha and

Jasmine on the swings. She felt faintly relieved that they weren't looking on.

Danny finished his run and crashed into a wall at some speed. At the last minute, he flung out his hands and managed to stop himself from ending up on the ground. Two seconds later, Paul did exactly the same thing and nearly knocked Danny flying. 'Watch it!' Danny protested.

'Should have got out of the way,' said Paul, grinning.

Danny was about to reply but his head suddenly lifted and he looked round. Megan felt a jolt. *Did he know I was watching?* she wondered. Danny's mouth curved up at the sides, and he beckoned her over. 'Megan Hirst,' he said. 'Good to see you.'

'That looked amazing,' said Megan.

Danny nodded. 'It's the best feeling ever, going that fast. You get an awesome buzz.'

'Like dancing,' suggested Megan. 'I get a buzz from dancing.'

'Yeah,' said Danny, examining the base of his board for any damage. 'So, you want another go?'

'Sure.' She stepped onto the board.

'Remember what I told you yesterday,' Danny said.

'I remember.' She lined up her feet the way he had

showed her. It felt just as wobbly as before, but at least this time she was prepared.

'Good,' said Danny. He smiled at her. 'Let's see what you can do.' He made her skate along the flat area a couple of times. 'Now you've got the hang of that,' he said, 'this is how you change direction . . .'

Megan wasn't convinced she had actually 'got the hang of it' at all, but she was pleased that Danny thought she was doing well. His gaze was fixed on her as she skated up and down – in fact, it was amazing she managed to stay on the board at all with his eyes on her! Paul watched for a while and then got bored and started practising some kind of jump. Megan caught sight of him out of the corner of her eye. 'How does he do that?' she asked curiously. 'It looks like the board is stuck to his feet when he jumps.'

'Deck, not board,' said Danny. 'It's called a deck.'

'Sorry.'

'I'll show you how,' he said, taking the board from her. 'It's called an ollie. It's about the most important move you can do on a skateboard.' He paused for a moment, and then leaped a couple of feet into the air. The skateboard rapped smartly on the ground and then lifted into the air with him, almost as though by magic.

'That's amazing,' said Megan. 'Why's it called an ollie?'

Danny shrugged. 'Some bloke called Ollie made it up, I guess. You want a go? I can show you how to do it.'

Megan laughed. 'I can't do that. I can hardly stay on the board as it is!'

'All beginners have to learn how to do an ollie,' said Danny. 'I'll talk you through it.'

Megan shook her head. 'This is going to be a disaster.' She stepped onto the board and Danny started to explain what she needed to do.

'You put your back foot as far back on the tail as you can . . . then you push off with the right, and slap the tail to the ground . . .'

Megan tried hard to follow his instructions, but her feet just didn't do what she wanted, and she ended up tripping over the board and stumbling gracelessly to the ground, twisting her ankle slightly as she did so. 'Ow.'

'You OK?' Danny was grinning. 'Not bad for a first try.'

Megan felt her ankle gingerly. 'It's all right, just a bit sore.'

Danny helped her up. 'Have another go,' he said encouragingly.

Megan laughed. 'No thanks. I'll sit down on this bench for a minute and wait for my ankle to stop throbbing.' She twirled it experimentally in the air. The ligaments felt tight, but she knew the ankle would be all right within a few hours.

Danny looked disappointed. 'Best thing to do after you fall is to get straight back on again.'

Megan grinned. 'Maybe that's why you have so many injuries?'

He gave a sudden laugh and Megan was astonished at how his face changed. It was as though the stormy grey of his eyes flashed with silver sunlight and for a second he looked almost like a different person. 'Yeah, maybe.'

Megan settled herself comfortably on the bench. 'Why don't you show me again? The ollie, I mean. It's easier to understand when you see someone else do it.'

'All right.' Danny's face lit up with enthusiasm and before too long, he was showing Megan all the other tricks he could do. Her head spun with words like 'kickflip', 'nollie' and 'goofy'. She tried to nod at the right times, and make appreciative noises, but after a while she realized that Danny didn't really need her to say anything at all. He just wanted her to watch – and that was something she was quite happy to do, because he truly was amazing. Paul came over to join them but although he was good, even Megan's inexperienced eye could see he didn't have the flair and daring of Danny.

'Don't you mind falling off?' she asked, after he had tried to demonstrate jumping a flight of concrete steps and landed heavily on his back.

'Nah,' he said, brushing down his jeans. 'You get used to it.' He grinned. 'Want to see my scars?' He pulled up a trouser leg. There was a livid red graze from the accident yesterday, but Danny pointed to a pale jagged line underneath. 'See this one here? I got it when I split my knee open. I was trying to jump a swimming pool and I crashed into the side. Couldn't walk for three weeks. Had twenty stitches.'

Megan stared at the jagged scar. 'Wow. That must have hurt.'

'Course.'

'But it didn't put you off?'

A slow smile crept over his face, and his eyes flashed silver again. 'No way. I live for this. Without skating – without bikes and speed and all that – I'd just crumble away and die. Do you know what I mean?'

Megan looked out over the skate park. It didn't hold the same appeal for her, but she recognized the passion in Danny's voice. He lived for it. She knew what that felt like. 'Yeah,' she said. 'I feel the same way about dancing.'

'Dancing?' Danny was momentarily startled. 'What, you mean like ballet?'

'No. I do ballroom dancing.' She saw the incomprehension on his face. 'Like – er – waltz? And rumba? Um . . . like on *Strictly Come Dancing*?'

'Oh.' Danny's face cleared. 'I get you. I don't really watch that stuff. Seems a bit lame to me.'

'That's because you don't know anything about it,' retorted Megan. 'It's just as difficult as your ollies and kickthings.'

He grinned at her. 'Whatever you say. Let me show you a manual. It's like a wheelie on a bike.' Off he went again.

I've never met anyone like him, Megan thought to herself. *It's weird because he loves skateboarding and I love dancing but it's as if we feel the same way about them. Almost like we're in two different worlds but are somehow connected.* A smile crept over her face as she wondered what her friends back home would think of Danny. What would *Jake* make of him? Danny and Jake were total opposites! Jake was quiet whereas Danny was brash; Jake was careful whereas Danny was wild . . . She watched him twist and flip his board along a ramp, and then trip and crash to the ground again.

'You finished yet?' called a voice, and Megan looked up to see Samantha and Jasmine heading towards them. Paul was busy trying to do something that looked like a twirl on his board at the far end of the park.

'No,' said Danny, sounding annoyed. 'Why?'

'Mum said she wanted us back for lunch,' said Samantha, glancing over at Megan. 'Oh, hello.'

'Hi.'

'Aunt Yvonne is coming, remember?'

Danny scowled. 'Don't see why I should be there. She doesn't like me anyway.'

Samantha rolled her eyes. 'It's not that she doesn't like you. But you didn't help last time by wearing that shirt with the bleeding skull on it. She thinks you're scary.'

Danny grinned. 'Even better.' He winked at Megan. 'I like being scary.' Megan couldn't help but smile back. 'What can I wear today?' he mused. 'The shirt with the big knife on it?'

'Don't you dare, Mum'll have a fit,' said Samantha. 'And besides, Aunt Yvonne usually gives us money, so don't do anything crazy.'

Danny's expression changed. 'That's right, I'd

forgotten. Maybe I can tap her for a tenner for new trucks.'

'You and your skateboard,' said Samantha. 'So are you coming then or not?'

Danny glanced at Paul. 'Oh, I'm off too, mate,' said Paul. 'Got some stuff to do for tomorrow.'

Samantha said to Paul, 'Am I coming round yours after school tomorrow?'

He shrugged. 'If you want.'

Megan felt puzzled. Why would Samantha be going round to Paul's house? Her jaw dropped when Paul walked over to Samantha and kissed her. Samantha accepted the kiss and waved goodbye before heading back up towards the playground. Jasmine turned and went too, having not said a single word.

Danny laughed at Megan's expression. 'What?'

'Are they . . . ? I mean, I didn't realize . . . Are they going out or something?'

'Or something,' agreed Danny. 'Can't think why. Samantha doesn't usually go for Paul's type. Think she's a bit off track at the moment, after what happened over the summer.'

Megan was going to ask what he meant, but he leaped onto the board and skimmed across the park again, calling, 'I'm going to do another kickflip, only this one on the end of the ramp!'

'Aren't you supposed to be going home?' she called back.

'In a minute!' He paused for a moment at the end of the park, his eyes fixed on the ramp, before pushing off and building up speed. As he hit the edge of the ramp, he kicked up with his feet and the board seemed magically to spin in mid-air before attaching itself to his feet again for a secure landing.

When Danny finally skidded to a halt in front of her, he did a silly bow. Megan laughed and said impulsively, 'Do you ever go other places? I mean, apart from hanging out here?'

He looked at her enquiringly. 'What do you mean?'

'Do you – go out?'

'Yeah. All kinds of places.' His gaze suddenly snapped up. 'You want to come?'

Megan felt breathless at the intensity of his gaze. His eyes had turned a stormy grey. It was almost like she was being pulled into some kind of cloud. 'Yes,' she said in a weak voice. 'I'd like to. If that's OK.'

He shrugged. 'Cool. I'll talk to the others.'

'Oh.' Megan took a breath. 'Could we go somewhere just us?' *What am I doing?* she wondered. The words were coming out of her mouth by themselves!

He looked surprised. 'Just us? Why?'

'Well – I'm not sure the girls like me that much.'

'You don't want to take any notice of them. Girls are weird.' He caught her eye. 'I don't mean you.'

Megan blushed. He thought she was different from other girls! A faint tingling started at the nape of her neck. 'But don't you think it would be nicer just us? We could talk properly.' Megan wasn't sure where this courage was coming from, but somehow she knew she really wanted to see Danny alone. 'Not a date,' she added hastily in case he'd be put off by the thought. 'Just a chance to get to know each other a bit more. After all, I haven't made many friends here yet.'

Danny studied her for a moment and then smiled. 'Sure. I'll take you somewhere really cool. I know just the place.'

♥

'How did it go?' Megan's dad asked as she let herself in the front door. 'You were only gone forty minutes after all that.'

'Was I?' Megan was taken aback. Was it really only forty minutes since she'd left the house? 'It felt like longer.'

'Are you a championship skateboarder now then?'

asked Bryan in a teasing voice. 'Got your ollies sorted from your nollies?'

'What?' said Megan, startled. 'How do you know about all that stuff?'

'I wasn't always a dad, you know,' said Bryan. 'I had a skateboard once. From a toy shop.'

Megan grinned. 'I don't think the boys I saw today would be impressed. They build their own – decks and trucks and everything.'

Bryan snorted with laughter. 'Now who's talking the language?'

They grinned at each other. 'I had a very nice time, thank you,' said Megan primly. 'Where's Mum and Owen?'

'Gone swimming,' said Bryan. 'Owen asked specially.'

For a moment, Megan felt disappointed. She loved swimming. And splashing around with Owen was good fun.

Bryan saw her face. 'We didn't know what time you'd be back. Owen had one of his manic moments. Your mum thought he should burn off some energy. Sorry.'

'It's OK.' She sat down on the sofa next to him. 'I can go next time.'

'So what did you do?' Bryan shuffled *The Sunday*

Times out of the way and turned to face her. 'Did you fall off?'

'Only once,' admitted Megan. 'I hurt my ankle a bit but it's OK now. Danny showed me some tricks while I was resting.'

'Danny?'

'This boy.'

'Ah . . .' said her dad in a knowing voice. 'A *boy*.'

Megan laughed. 'He's really nice, Dad. And amazing on a skateboard – I mean, really mind-boggling.'

Bryan grinned. 'Let me guess – he's also incredibly good-looking and was very nice to you all the time you were there.'

Megan flushed. 'Dad . . .'

He held up his hands. 'Sorry, sorry. Didn't mean to embarrass you. So, are you going back again? To – uh – see Danny?'

'We might be sort of going out somewhere together . . . ' mumbled Megan. 'Maybe.'

'Say no more,' said her dad. He patted her on the back. 'I hope you have a lovely time.'

♥

Megan knew it was Jake when her mobile rang, but when she answered it, all she could hear was laughing. 'Jake? Jake, what's going on?'

'AHAHAHA!' Jake laughed loudly in her ear. 'AHAHAHAAAA! Seriously, though, I'm crying with laughter here.'

'Why?' Megan felt the corners of her own mouth creep up. 'What's so funny?'

There was a pause and then Jake said, 'You on a skateboard! AHAHAHAAAA!'

'Oh ha ha, yes it's all hilarious,' said Megan sarcastically. 'Have *you* ever been on one?'

'I *have* actually,' said Jake, stopping laughing as suddenly as he had started. 'For about five minutes. It didn't go anywhere, so I got off.'

Megan laughed despite herself. 'You idiot.'

'So, how did you do?'

'Not too bad,' Megan told him proudly. 'I only fell off once.'

'Was that when it started moving?'

Megan blew a loud raspberry down the phone. 'You are impossible. I won't tell you anything else about it.'

'Fine. I've got news to tell you instead.'

'Really? What kind of news?'

Jake sounded amused. 'You know that drinky thing we had to go to the other evening? With the new people next door?'

'Yeah.'

'Well, it turned out to be this really mad evening. We were there till one o'clock in the morning!'

Megan nearly dropped the phone. 'What? On a *school night*? Bet your mum loved that!'

Jake chuckled. 'You'd be surprised. She was playing charades with a party hat on her head.'

'No!'

'But that's not the strangest thing,' Jake continued. 'They're knocking through the kitchen and lounge wall, and they've put a hot tub in the conservatory!'

'A *hot tub*?' Megan clutched the phone. 'You're *not* going to tell me you spent the evening in a hot tub?'

'No. It'd only just arrived that day, there wasn't any water in it or anything. I did sit in it for a minute but then Skye told me I might damage it.'

'Who's Skye?'

'She's the girl next door. She's got a brother – get this – he's called Jasper.'

Megan giggled. 'They're called Skye and Jasper? Wow, they're going to stick out a bit in Milton.'

'I know. Skye told me she's already had some kids at school making up songs about her.'

'Oh, that's nasty.'

'Ah well, they'll get bored soon. I told her not to worry. She's really nice. Same age as us.'

Megan felt suspicious. 'Do you *fancy* her, Jake?'

'Of course not.' Jake's response was just a little too quick, Megan thought. 'She's just a friend.'

'Riiiight.'

'Why do you girls do that? I haven't asked you if you fancy Danny Boy, have I?'

'Don't call him Danny Boy.'

'Anyway, it doesn't matter.' Jake took a breath. 'Listen, there's something else. Mum and I were talking the other day and she said maybe I could come down and visit you guys in half-term. What do you think?'

'Oh!' Megan felt a smile sweep across her face. 'That would be fab! Half-term's only about three weeks away, isn't it? That would be amazing!'

Jake sounded a little relieved. 'Good. I wasn't sure if . . . I mean, I thought maybe you might be busy with your new friends or something.'

'Are you kidding?' Megan laughed. 'You're my best friend. It would be so cool if you came to see us. Would you stay for a bit?'

'Yeah, a couple of nights, I think. If that's OK.'

'I'm sure it'll be fine. I'll talk to Mum.'

'My mum says if you can meet my train, too . . .

there's a direct one from Milton to Parchester, which is kind of handy.'

Megan grinned. 'We can get it sorted. Oh, wow! I can't believe you're coming to stay! We're going to have such a brilliant time!'

Chapter 6

you're GOING OUT WITH HIM?

'I *am* getting better, aren't I?' Mari gazed anxiously at Megan. 'You would tell me, wouldn't you, if I was completely hopeless?'

Megan laughed. 'You're making good progress, Mari. You just need to listen to the rhythm a bit more. Try to feel the beat.'

Mari glanced around the studio. It was the end of the class and Megan had spent most of it trying to teach Mari the short routine Corinne had given them. 'Everyone else can do it better than me.'

Megan pulled off her shoes. 'No they can't. You're imagining things. And you're doing really well in those shoes.'

'They help,' confessed Mari. 'I can sort of imagine I'm a proper dancer, you know. Thanks so much for lending them to me.' She glanced at the shoes in Megan's hands. 'Are you sure you don't want these back? Only, the ones you've got now . . .'

'Are very comfortable,' finished Megan, grinning. 'Don't worry. They're not sparkly silver like yours but they're fine. I have another silver pair but they're for best only.'

'Best what?'

'Well, when I do competitions and things like that.'

Mari shook her head in awe. 'Wow. Competitions. I can't imagine dancing in front of anyone, let alone competing.'

Megan felt a pang. She had always entered competitions with Jake. Now, even those shoes were a reminder of the old days in Milton. When was she going to find a class that was more suited to her level? Because nice though it was, this salsa class wasn't challenging her in any way – unless it was as a teacher!

As if she'd read Megan's mind, Mari suddenly said, 'I don't suppose . . .' and then stopped.

'What?'

'Well, I was wondering . . .' Mari chewed her lip for a moment and then rushed on with, 'You're such a good teacher, Megan, I was wondering if you'd give me a bit more help. Outside classes, I mean.'

Megan was surprised. 'Outside classes? You mean, practise on our own?'

'Yes. I just don't want to hold everyone else back.'

Mari's face was beginning to turn red. 'Of course, if you're busy . . .'

Megan laughed. 'Don't be silly. I'd love to help out a bit.'

Corinne, who was passing, overheard this. 'Good idea. You're a good teacher, Megan. Have you ever thought of doing it as a career?'

'No,' said Megan, taken aback. 'Not really.'

'Well, it's just a thought. Come on, you two, I need to lock up this room.'

Megan and Mari headed towards the front entrance, discussing when and where they could meet up. 'My house is tiny,' said Mari abruptly. 'We'd only be able to take three steps in any direction. How much room have you got?'

'Quite a lot,' replied Megan, considering. 'If we rolled back the rug in the lounge . . .'

'Whereabouts is your house?'

'Just three minutes round the corner. Listen,' said Megan as a thought struck her, 'why don't you come back that way now and I'll point it out to you?'

Mari nodded. 'Good idea. Then I can come knocking on your door one evening!'

They approached the skate park together, and Megan felt her heart skip a beat as she spotted Danny practising ollies in the middle of the concrete. On an impulse, she turned to Mari. 'You see that boy over there?' she whispered.

'Which one? The tall one with the dark hair?'

'Yes. He's teaching me to skateboard.'

Mari looked astonished. 'He's what? You're learning to skateboard?'

Megan nodded, eyes sparkling. 'Well, sort of. He's amazing, Mari. He can do all these jumps and tricks and things.'

'I'll bet he can. He's *very* cute too.' Mari raised her eyebrows. 'How do you know him?'

'I bumped into him one day. Literally. We crashed into each other.'

'Wow. And so now he's teaching you to skateboard.' Mari nudged her friend. 'Did you pretend to be interested so that you could talk to him?'

'I *am* interested! Skateboarding is kind of fun.'

Mari grinned. 'Bet it's more fun when you've got a good-looking boy teaching you!'

Megan blushed. 'Well, that helps, I suppose. But he is really amazing. I mean, look at that! How does he do it?'

'Oh dear,' said Mari, smirking, 'you have got it bad. Shouldn't you dash down there now? Aren't you afraid someone else is going to become his pet pupil?'

'I hadn't even thought of that,' said Megan, startled.

'But then there are these two girls who hang around him. One of them's his sister. They're not very friendly. They nearly scared me off.'

Mari laughed. 'Nice. He must be worth it, to put up with them!'

'He is. Well, I like him. And I'm sure the girls are nice really. It's just taking a while to get to know them.' A movement behind Danny caught her eye. 'There they are. Those two, just coming down the steps from the playground.'

Mari glanced across, amused. Then, suddenly, she stiffened all over. Her eyes turned hard and cold. 'Those two girls?' she said icily. 'The blonde one and her friend?'

'Yes. The blonde one is his sister. Danny's sister, I mean.'

Mari grabbed her arm, and Megan jumped at the tightness of her grip. 'But that's *Samantha*,' she hissed.

Megan was startled. 'Samantha, yes, that's right. Do you know her?'

'Samantha Brooks,' said Mari urgently. 'That's her! That's the girl who injured Fliss in the play!'

Megan gaped. '*What?*'

Mari pulled Megan back towards the arts centre and out of sight of the skate park. 'Oh my God, have you not been listening to a word I said? That's Sam-antha Brooks! She's only the most evil cow-bag ever!'

'But . . . but . . .'

'And you've been *hanging out with her?*' Mari sud-denly dropped Megan's arm, a horrified expression on her face.

'I didn't know it was her!' protested Megan, sud-denly defensive though she had no idea why. 'I've only just moved in! How would I know anything about what happened?' A sudden thought struck her. Danny had said something about Samantha being 'off track' since what happened in the summer . . .

Mari was glaring at the ground. 'Megan, you've got to stay away from her. She's a nasty piece of work.'

Megan felt uncomfortable. 'Well, it's not that easy, if I'm going out with her brother.'

Mari actually took a step backwards. 'You're GOING OUT WITH HIM?'

'Not like that, not like that! Mari, you've got it all wrong!' Megan gabbled. 'We're not going out like boyfriend and girlfriend, it's just I only ever see him at the skate park and I said it would be nice to go somewhere just the two of us and so he said he'd take me somewhere really cool and we could . . .' Her voice trailed off under Mari's steely expression. 'He's really nice,' she ended lamely.

'He can't be nice,' Mari said in a decided tone. 'He's a Brooks. He's Samantha's brother.'

'Exactly,' said Megan, feeling a little more sure of herself. 'He's her brother. He's not *her*. I mean, you can't say just because she's nasty that he is too. Have you even met him before?'

'No,' admitted Mari.

'Well, then.'

Mari shifted from foot to foot. 'But if you hang out with him, you have to hang out with her,' she said. 'That's what you said. She's always around.'

Megan felt frustrated. 'Well, what do you want me to do? I like him. He's really cool on a skateboard and he wants to teach me. She's not very friendly, but I don't have to be friends with her, do I?' She took a breath. 'Look, Mari, I know why you feel the way you do, but I only just moved here. I haven't got many friends yet. Danny's been nice to me. I don't want to stop seeing him.'

Mari sighed. 'Sorry, Megan. I didn't mean to go off the deep end. I know I put my foot in it sometimes. It's just that Samantha and I – we have a bit of history, let's say.'

'I know, but . . .'

'And I will *never* forgive her for what she did to Fliss,' Mari went on. 'But I don't know Danny at all.

He could be nothing like her. And you have a right to be friends with whoever you want, of course you do.' She glanced back towards the skate park. 'Just be careful, that's all. You don't want to get on the wrong side of Samantha.'

Megan grinned. 'All right. And thanks for looking out for me.'

'He's waving at you,' said Mari. 'I should go.'

'No, don't.' Megan grabbed her arm. 'I'm showing you where I live, remember?' She waved back at Danny and then firmly turned away, although she really wanted to run over to him. 'I can talk to him tomorrow.'

'I'm impressed,' joked Mari as they walked away from the skate park. 'You may be smitten, but you're staying strong. Good on you, girl.'

'Mari,' said Megan affectionately, 'you are an idiot.'

Chapter 7

Let's do it again!

Megan's jaw dropped. She'd never seen anything like this before.

'Cool, isn't it?' said Danny enthusiastically.

Everywhere she looked, Megan saw red and white stripes, rubber tyres, steel beams, tarmac . . . And the *noise*! 'I never realized go-karting was so loud!' she said, raising her voice.

'What?' Danny called back. 'Oh, yeah! I know, it's the engines!'

Megan wanted to put her hands over her ears. She could see them, the low-slung karts, racing around the track. The whole building was like some giant aircraft hangar, and the ceiling was criss-crossed with what looked like scaffolding and steel struts. Big banners advertising brand names – Pirelli, Dunlop, Ferrari – adorned the walls. To her right was the reception desk, and beyond that a seated area with a TV screen. The other side of this was a snack bar, and several people were already seated and tucking into pizzas, laughing and joking around with their friends.

But the really fascinating sight was the track itself. Bordered by concrete and tyres, striped red and white, it snaked tightly round corners and even up and over itself. The karts whizzed dizzyingly past, some overtaking, the odd one crashing into the barrier with a body-stunning jolt. Megan felt her mouth go dry. The drivers were completely anonymous, dressed identically in boiler suits and full helmets. She glanced at Danny. His face was lit up as he watched the karts. His eyes seemed to be fizzing with sparks. Megan felt a slight quiver somewhere in the pit of her stomach. It was the first time she'd been somewhere with a boy who wasn't Jake. And Danny was so definitely *not* like Jake, she wasn't sure exactly how to behave.

'Are you sure . . .' Megan started to say, and then swallowed. 'Are you sure it's safe? I mean, it looks kind of dangerous.'

Danny laughed. 'That's half the fun. Come on, let's get you kitted up.' He glanced at her feet. 'Good, you wore trainers like I said. You just need the rest of the stuff.' He lifted his right hand and waved his helmet at her. 'I brought my own.'

Megan followed him to the reception desk, where

the assistant booked them in and looked her up and down critically before passing over a boiler suit and helmet. 'Take them to the briefing area,' he said. 'Someone will show you how to put them on.'

'I can help her,' said Danny. 'I've been here before.'

The assistant shook his head. 'Sorry, mate. Everyone has to sit through the briefing. Doesn't matter how many times you've been.'

Danny tapped his hand on the desk impatiently. 'It takes time away from racing.'

The assistant grinned. 'Don't worry, we won't dock your track time. It's just the rules, mate.'

Danny rolled his eyes and turned to Megan. 'Come on then. Let's go and do the health-and-safety stuff.'

Megan sat clutching her suit and helmet as a burly man in a red fleece explained to a small group of them how the karts worked, how to speed up and brake, what to do if you crashed and how to overtake. Megan decided straight away she wouldn't be overtaking anyone! Her legs felt oddly as though they belonged to someone else. And her mind was playing strange tricks on her too. She had a ridiculous impulse to put her hand on Danny's leg for reassurance as she sat next to him. How embarrassing would that be! Megan gripped her suit even tighter, her knuckles turning white.

'Now,' said the burly bloke, whose name badge said 'Bodge', 'as you can appreciate, this is a high-speed sport. Although we take all reasonable steps to keep you safe, it's up to you to take final responsibility. Injuries, though rare here, can and do happen. If anyone has a back or neck problem, you can't drive. Simple as that – you need to be in tip-top condition to race.' He glared at them all. 'No heroics. If you don't think you're safe to drive, then don't. It's not just your-self you could be putting at risk.' He reached behind him and produced a sheaf of papers. 'These are your disclaimer forms. You need to sign them to say you're in good health.' He started handing them out. 'Most important thing is to have fun though. Racing is a real buzz, and if you haven't tried it before, you're in for a treat!' He grinned as he handed Megan her sheet.

Megan tried to smile back but her facial muscles didn't seem to be working. Her head was swimming with everything Bodge had just said. *Injuries?* 'What sort of injuries?' she whispered to Danny, who was struggling to get his pen to work. 'I mean, does he mean serious ones or just cuts and grazes and things like that?' The words were tumbling out of her in a nervous rush. 'How often do people get hurt? Once a week? Once a *day*?'

'What?'

'Has anyone actually *died*?' Megan asked urgently.

Danny turned to her, amused. 'What are you on about? I don't know. Don't think so – we'd have heard, wouldn't we? Why? You scared?'

Megan opened her mouth to say, 'Of course I'm scared, I'm so terrified I don't think I can stand up,' but the words froze in her throat. Danny was looking at her as though being frightened was a completely alien notion to him. *It can't be that dangerous*, Megan told herself, *otherwise they wouldn't let people do it. And Danny brought me here to share something he likes.* She glanced again at the track. The steady *whumm-whumm* of the engines thumped through her head. They were whizzing round so fast. What if she broke a leg or an arm, or . . . her *neck*? She might never be able to dance again!

But you wanted to try something new, Megan scolded herself. *Just because it's a bit scary, you can't back out now. Besides, Danny would think you were a complete wimp.* And, she realized, she definitely didn't want him to think that.

She took a breath and turned to Danny. 'Raring to go!' she said in what she hoped was a convincing voice.

He beamed back at her. 'You're going to love it.'

Bodge came round to each person and checked

they'd put on their helmets correctly. Megan felt very silly in her boiler suit, which was about two sizes too large for her. The helmet was very tight, and she wished she'd taken out her ponytail because the band was digging uncomfortably into the back of her head.

'You look really cute,' Danny said, regarding her in her outfit.

Megan blushed hotly. 'I look ridiculous.'

'No you don't.' There was a strange look in Danny's silver eyes. 'You look cute.'

Megan tried to laugh casually, but a strand of hair caught in her mouth and made her cough. *I must look like such an idiot!*

'Gloves,' said Bodge bluntly, shoving some into Megan's hands. 'You two ready then?'

Megan followed the rest of the group to the side of the track. A bell shrilled, and the racing go-karts zoomed, one by one, into the pit. Their drivers got out, shouting and jeering at each other. 'Ready?' asked Danny in an excited voice.

Not really! thought Megan, but there was no time to think any more because she was climbing into her kart and Bodge was pointing out the controls he had explained earlier. The instructions whirled around Megan's head and she was just about to say, 'Sorry, could you repeat that?' when another bell shrilled and Bodge jumped to safety as the engines roared into life and the karts suddenly shot off around the track.

Megan saw Danny's kart disappear round the first corner and panic rose in her throat. Desperately, she tried to remember what she had been told. Push down on the accelerator . . . The kart leaped forward, and Megan frantically gripped the wheel as the engine roared behind her.

The noise filled her whole body; it felt as though every internal organ was vibrating to the noise of the engine. Megan had no idea how fast she was going, but the low-slung seat made it feel very fast indeed. She swung the wheel desperately from one side to the other, and the kart zigzagged across the track. Other karts zoomed past her. One or two of the drivers made rude gestures to her as they passed, but Megan couldn't hear what they shouted. *Come on*, she told herself. *It's not that hard. Everyone else can do it. Get a grip!* She took a breath, grasped the wheel firmly with her gloved hands, and pressed down gradually on the pedal.

The kart gathered speed along a straight. Megan felt the shudder of the seat and eased off the accelerator as she approached the corner. The wheel turned smoothly and she navigated the bend without mishap.

Two more karts zoomed past her, but she ignored them. It was just a matter of practice, wasn't it? Just like dance – the more you did it, the better you got.

After a couple of laps, Megan felt more confident and increased her speed. 'Whoa!' The breath whooshed out of her, and she felt a tingle of excitement in her feet. 'That's fast! Wheeee!' Eagerly, she pushed down harder and felt the world rush past her even faster. But there was a corner coming up, and suddenly she was going too fast to turn . . .

Megan skidded across the track and crashed heavily into the wall of tyres. A kart just behind her caught the back wheel and spun off too, though the driver regained control quickly and sped off, shouting something at Megan.

Megan sat winded for a moment, her head fizzing. Was she hurt? No, nothing was aching or sore. That had been a massive jolt – but she was uninjured. 'Wow!' she said out loud. And then, almost without knowing, she revved the engine. 'Let's do it again!'

Round and round she drove, getting faster and more confident all the time. And then – yes! With only minutes left before the end of the session, Megan overtook another kart! 'Wheeee!' she screamed as she zoomed past. This was the most amazing thing she'd ever done!

By the time the bell rang shrilly, Megan felt as though she had been driving all her life. Expertly, she steered the kart into the pit. What a shame it had to stop just as she was getting the hang of it! She sat there for a moment, trying to slow her breathing.

'You OK?' came Danny's voice. He leaned over and undid her harness for her. 'There you go.'

'Thanks.' Megan pulled off her helmet and grinned up at him. 'I'm not sure I can get out of this.'

He laughed. 'Give me your hand.' With a strong heave, he helped Megan up. Her legs felt stiff and strangely tingly, as though they could still feel the engine beneath them. 'You're all pink.'

'Am I?' Megan pulled the band from her ponytail and shook out her hair. She rubbed the back of her head ruefully. 'Remind me to have my hair loose next time.'

'I think you should wear it down like that more often,' said Danny, staring at her. 'It suits you.'

'Thanks.' She smiled. Why did everything suddenly seem so much more vibrant, more vivid?

'Move along, folks,' said Bodge from their left. 'Next group wants to get in. Don't forget to take your kit back to reception.'

Danny took Megan's hand. 'Come on. Got to get out of the way.'

The two of them headed back to the front desk where they wriggled out of their boiler suits and Megan handed back the items she'd borrowed.

'What did you think?' Danny turned to Megan. 'Did you like it?'

Megan looked at him. His eyes were alight, as though there were a flame burning inside them. His cheeks were flushed and he gazed at her with that strange intensity. *He really loves this*, Megan realized. *He loves it, lives for it. His whole being is exploding with passion for racing.*

She beamed at him. 'You know what? I thought I was going to hate it, but I love it! It's amazing!'

His face split into a smile. 'I knew it!'

'I want another go,' said Megan. 'But maybe not just now, because my legs are all shaky.'

'That gets better,' Danny told her. 'The first time is scary, but your legs won't shake next time.' He put an arm around her shoulders. 'Let's get some food.'

Megan nodded, suddenly realizing she was ravenous. The snack bar was along one side of the track. 'What's good?'

'Pizza!' said Danny confidently. He dug around in his pocket and produced a twenty-pound note. 'Have what you like, my mum's paying.'

'Oh, that's nice of her.'

'She doesn't actually know,' Danny said with a laugh. 'I sort of borrowed it from her purse.'

'You didn't!' Megan stared at him.

He held up his hands. 'Don't worry, I'll tell her when I get home.' He laughed again. 'She's used to it anyway. And I always pay her back. Right, what do you want?'

'What are you having?'

'Meat feast,' said Danny promptly. 'I always have a meat feast after racing.'

'Oh, right. Can I have the four-cheese pizza then?'

'Sure. You go get us a table.'

'OK.'

'Near the track,' Danny called after her. 'Then we can watch the racing.'

Megan sat down at a table right at the edge of the track. The next group session was well under way and the karts were zipping around the track at speed. Megan couldn't quite believe that had been her just a few minutes ago. And to think that when she first came in, the noise gave her a headache and she was shaking with fear! Now she gazed intently at the track, drinking in the speed, the noise, the wildness of it all. The whole place seemed to suit Danny's personality. He was wild and fast and loud too. She felt uneasy that he'd taken the money from his mum's purse without asking. But maybe that's just how things were in his family? And he *did* say he always paid her back . . .

Danny joined her a few minutes later, clutching two Cokes and a ticket for the pizzas. 'They'll yell out our number when they're ready,' he told her. 'I got you a Coke.'

'Thanks.'

'So . . .' He sat back on his chair and looked at her with that intensity in his eyes again. 'What was it you liked most about racing?'

Megan glanced out across the track and smiled. 'I don't know. All of it, I guess.'

'The speed?'

'I wasn't sure about the speed to start with,' she admitted. 'It seems so fast when you're that close to the ground. Everything whizzes by in a blur. And the engines are so powerful.'

Danny nodded, his eyes gleaming. 'I know. Cool, isn't it?'

'It is, but it was kind of scary to start with. And then I got a grip, and it all got easier. I even overtook someone!'

Danny laughed at her pride. 'I knew you'd understand. Racing is awesome. Winning is just the best feeling ever.'

'I think I'm a long way from winning.'

'Come a few more times and you will, I bet.' He hesitated a moment. 'Most girls go all stupid over things like this. You know, they start squealing or going on about how they can't possibly, it's too scary. But not you.'

Megan blushed. 'Well, it was nice to try something different.' She tried to sound casual, and not at all as though she had been scared stiff only an hour before.

'That's what I mean. You're up for trying new stuff and you don't mind having a go.' He leaned forward. 'You're a cool kind of girl.'

Megan didn't know where to look. He thought she was cool! 'I think you're cool too,' she mumbled, and instantly regretted it. What a dumb thing to say!

But Danny just smiled. 'See? We should definitely hang out together again.'

Megan beamed. Right now, there was nothing she'd like more!

By the time their number was called for the pizzas, Megan felt as though they were getting on brilliantly. She'd pretended to Danny that it wasn't really a date, but inside she felt they had such a connection, it might as well be. Danny came back with the pizzas and Megan was pleasantly surprised.

'They look really good. I thought somewhere like this . . .'

'. . . would do cheap rubbish,' finished Danny.

'Well, yeah.'

He laughed. 'You say what you think. Just like me. It's cool.'

Megan blushed again and tried to hide her confusion by tucking into her pizza. For a few minutes they ate without speaking, though Megan noticed that Danny's eyes were constantly drawn to the karts whizzing round the track. 'You really love it, don't you?' she commented.

'Huh?'

'You've asked me – now I'm asking you. What is it *you* like the most?'

Danny wiped his mouth with the back of his hand and paused for a moment. 'I like going fast. I like wheels.'

'Why?'

He shrugged. 'I dunno. Maybe because feet seem so – kind of useless. You know? You can only walk or run. Wheels, now . . . you can make them spin or skid or screech.'

'Is it about power?' Megan persisted. 'Or being in control?'

Danny laughed. 'More about being *out* of control. I

109

love that feeling when you know something's so close to disaster . . . and then you bring it back, and you've survived. Awesome!'

'Like being on a rollercoaster?' suggested Megan.

'Nah, rollercoasters are tame,' replied Danny, taking another bite of pizza. 'You know you're never going to fall off. Skateboards, now, or bikes . . . you never know what's going to happen.'

Megan nodded thoughtfully. 'I see.' She smiled. 'It's very different from what I'm used to.'

'What are you used to?'

'Dancing,' Megan said simply.

'Oh yeah, you said.' Danny glanced at the track again. 'I can see why this is different.'

Megan felt anxious to explain. 'It's not about speed or winning, so much. It's about control and perfection. And beauty.' She blushed slightly.

Danny separated out his last two pieces of pizza. 'Sounds a bit – well . . . lame to me.'

'It's about skill,' countered Megan. 'Just like driving is about skill. You work hard to get good at it.'

Danny nodded. 'Fair enough. You wouldn't catch me in tights though.'

Megan rolled her eyes. 'Why does everyone go on about the tights? It's not just the clothes, you know.'

Danny chuckled. 'You are so easy to wind up. You want that last piece of pizza?'

'Yes I do, so hands off.'

He laughed again and Megan found herself smiling back. Being with Danny was so amazing. It was as though the real world didn't exist. At least . . . was it really that? Or was it more that he was the most *alive* person she'd ever met? He was almost *more* real than real, if that made any sense . . . 'I've never met anyone like you,' she blurted out, and then felt horrified. What a ridiculous thing to say!

Danny was amused. 'Don't they have karts and skateboards oop north?'

'Very funny. Of course they do. I've just never been karting before.' *Especially not with a boy*, she added silently to herself. An involuntary chuckle escaped her at the thought of Jake on a skateboard.

'What?'

'Nothing. Just thinking about this boy back home.'

'Yeah?' Danny crumpled his serviette into a ball. 'Boring, was he?'

Megan laughed again. 'Compared to you? Yes, I guess so.'

Danny nodded, satisfied. Megan felt a tiny twinge of betrayal. She had never thought of Jake as boring before, had she? *But then I hadn't met Danny,* she thought. *And now, suddenly, life looks a lot more exciting.*

'You want to come out with me again next weekend?'

A thrill shot through Megan. 'Back here?'

He shook his head. 'No. There's a BMX meet just outside Parchester. Paul and I are going, and I guess the girls will tag along too. You want to come?'

Megan frowned. 'What's a BMX meet? Will I be standing around getting bored?'

Danny grinned. 'It's racing. And if you want, I'll let you have a go on my bike.'

Megan picked a small ball of fluff off her jumper and tried to sound cool. 'I'll think about it.'

But she already knew she would go.

Chapter 8

we're desperate for gossip!

'Go-karting?' Suki said, wrinkling her little button-shaped nose. 'That sounds a bit . . . boyish.'

'You know, I really enjoyed it,' Megan told her as they sat down for lunch at school. 'Jacket potato and cheese, yum.'

'You know, tuna's much better for you than cheese,' said Suki, distracted for a moment. 'If you want to keep a dancer's shape, I mean. Have you heard about the Atkins Diet?'

'No,' replied Megan, determined to keep control of the conversation. 'Have you ever been go-karting?'

Suki shook her head. 'I wouldn't dare. What if I broke my leg or something? What about my dance career? I'm amazed you risked it. But then you're not so serious about your dancing as I am about mine.'

'It was fun,' said Megan, ignoring this last

comment. 'I didn't think I'd like it but it was amazing.'

'And who was this boy you went with again?' asked Suki.

'His name's Danny. He's not from our school. I met him at the skate park. He does skateboarding and things.'

Suki had a funny expression on her face. 'He sounds a bit . . . well, I wouldn't have thought he was your type.'

Megan felt faintly annoyed. 'What do you mean?'

Suki shrugged. 'No offence or anything. I just didn't realize you were that sort of girl. You know, into skating and dangerous sports.'

'You never know until you try them,' Megan said defensively. 'I just never had the chance to try them before. And I like them – it. Go-karting, I mean. It's brilliant fun. And I'd definitely go again.'

Suki shrugged. 'Cool. Whatever suits you.'

Megan attacked the rest of her jacket potato with some force.

Mari's response couldn't have been more different. 'Go-karting, wow! I went once. I was really, really awful at it. I just froze up, couldn't do anything. In the end they had to get me out again because I was causing an obstruction.' She laughed. 'I'd go again but I think I might have been banned.'

Megan grinned. 'Maybe you just didn't go with the right people.'

'You're offering to take me, are you?'

Megan raised her eyebrows. 'If you want to, yeah. It'd be cool!'

The two of them were practising in Megan's front room. Megan's mum was feeding Owen his tea in the kitchen but every now and then he escaped to come and see what the two girls were doing. This was one of those moments, and Megan and Mari looked up to see a little face peering round the door.

'Can I have a go?' asked Owen.

'Course you can,' said Mari, just as Megan opened her mouth to refuse. 'Bet you'll be way better than me though.'

Owen nodded. 'It's only because I've got more rhythm than you.'

'Owen!' Megan spluttered. 'You can't say things like that!'

'Why not?'

'Oh, I don't mind,' said Mari. 'He's right, anyway. I can't even clap in time.'

Owen came to join them in the middle of the

floor. Megan switched on the music again and she and Mari started to practise. Owen joined in, although his dancing consisted mostly of twirling round and round in circles until he got dizzy and fell over.

'Owen!' Megan's mum came to the doorway. 'I thought you were going to finish the rest of your banana and ice cream?'

Owen shook his head. 'I'm too busy dancing, Mummy.'

'Ooh, bananas and ice cream,' said Mari. 'One of my favourites.'

'You can have it then,' offered Owen generously. 'I haven't spitted in it much.'

Mari burst out laughing. 'That's very kind of you, Owen, but I think maybe I'll pass.'

'Would you girls like banana and ice cream too?' Nicola asked. She winked. 'You can have your *own* bowls and spoons. You've been practising for half an hour now. It looks like hard work.'

Mari grinned. 'Dancing and dessert. Music to my ears.'

♥

Jake seemed pleased, though Megan thought she detected something restrained in his voice.

'I think it's great,' he said over the phone. 'Great that you had such a good time, I mean.'

Megan waited. Wasn't he going to say anything else? 'I was really surprised,' she said, when Jake didn't continue. 'I mean, not just about the go-karting, but about Danny. We have quite a lot in common, though you wouldn't have thought it.'

'That's nice,' said Jake.

'He's really into this racing stuff. And you know that buzz we get from dancing? He gets the same thing from racing, or skateboarding, stuff like that.'

Jake laughed, though it didn't sound quite natural. 'At least dancing isn't dangerous.'

'No . . .' A thought suddenly struck Megan. 'You know it's all quite safe though, don't you? I mean, I was wearing a helmet and everything. And I had to sign a form to say I didn't have any injuries. You don't have to worry about me.'

'That's not quite what I meant,' said Jake, but he wouldn't say any more.

'So,' said Megan, sitting cross-legged on her bed, 'have you talked to your mum again about coming down for half-term? Because my mum said it would be a great idea. We could meet you at the train station, and you can stay in the spare room. It's not actually painted yet – well, it is, but it's this horrible yellow colour at the moment – and I can take you round Parchester and show you the Alexander Arts Centre where I go for the salsa, and we can go to the cinema . . .' Megan trailed off, suddenly aware that Jake wasn't saying anything. 'And it'll be just like old times,' she finished lamely.

'Yeah,' said Jake, though he wasn't exactly jumping with excitement. 'Well, maybe.'

'You *are* coming, aren't you?' Megan felt a sharp pang. She hadn't realized until that moment how much she was looking forward to seeing Jake again.

'Yeah, yeah,' he said hastily. 'Of course I'm coming. Yeah. Can't wait.'

But when Megan hung up, she had an uneasy feeling that something was wrong.

♥

'Have you heard from him?' Mari asked.

Corinne was running late, so the girls were sitting along the wall of the studio and chatting. Megan flushed. 'Not exactly. I saw him yesterday at the skate park but we didn't have time to talk.'

A girl with cropped blonde hair sitting nearby turned curiously. 'You're all red, Megan. Who are you talking about?'

'Ooh, Jackie, you have no idea of the excitement,' Mari said mischievously. 'Megan had a *date* on Saturday.'

Jackie gaped. 'No! Really?' The two girls next to her turned to listen.

'Gather round, gather round,' said Mari, with a grin. 'Megan is about to reveal all.'

Megan wanted to fall through the floor. 'Mari, what are you *doing*?'

'Megan, don't you realize you've got the most exciting news of all of us?' said Mari. She addressed the other girls. 'How many of you had a date over the weekend?'

The girls looked at each other. Nobody raised a hand.

'There, see?' said Mari. 'We're desperate for gossip!'

'But I already told you yesterday . . .'

'Yes, but your little brother kept interrupting,' Mari pointed out. 'And I never got to hear the juicy bits.'

'There aren't any juicy bits!' cried Megan.

'Hey,' said Jackie, 'this is no good. You have to start at the beginning. Tell us everything.'

Megan was agonized. She looked around at the rest of the girls, who were all gazing at her expectantly. Alys was chewing the end of her brown plait, she was so fascinated. 'I don't know what to say.'

'I'll start off for you,' said Mari comfortably. 'Megan has been learning to skateboard. No, don't laugh, she really has! And her teacher is the very good-looking Danny Brooks.'

Jackie whispered something to Alys.

'What was that?' asked Mari.

'Oh, nothing,' said Jackie hastily. 'I was just saying . . . he's kind of obsessed with bikes and things. But he is *very* good-looking.'

'Who is he?' asked a girl called Naomi, baffled. 'I've never heard of him.'

Jackie turned to her. 'He's always at the skate park. He's the tall one with the black hair. You know. Kind of gothic-looking.'

'Oh!' Naomi's expression cleared. 'I think I've seen him around.' She stared at Megan. 'And he asked you out? Wow.'

'Well,' said Megan, uncomfortable, 'I sort of asked *him* out.'

There was a collective gasp of admiration. 'That's amazing,' breathed someone. 'I would never dare . . .' muttered someone else. Megan felt a little twinge of pride. It hadn't really occurred to her that she'd done something no one else would have had the courage to do.

'He's done some modelling, you know,' Jackie offered. 'In a magazine. I saw it once.'

'So has his sister,' said Alys.

Mari's face darkened. 'We don't talk about her. She's top of my Never Speak To List. But she's got nothing to do with this. Megan went out with Danny at the weekend.'

'It's not quite how it sounds,' Megan tried to explain. 'It was only that I've been hanging out with him and the others, and I said it would be nice to go somewhere just the two of us . . .' She tailed off.

'*So*,' said Mari meaningfully, 'tell us everything. And don't leave anything out this time.'

'Oh, all right.' Megan was embarrassed but there was something exciting about having everyone sitting round and hanging on her every word. It was nice to be the centre of attention for once. And some of the girls looked quite envious. Presumably she wasn't the only one who had noticed how good-looking Danny was. 'Well, he took me go-karting.'

Alys looked blank. 'What's that?'

'It's like cars,' Megan explained. 'I mean, they've got engines. Like mini-cars, I suppose.'

'Like dodgems?'

'Not exactly. You drive them round a track. In a race.'

Alys looked impressed. 'Wow. Like Formula One.'

Jackie rolled her eyes in amusement. 'You know nothing! Haven't you ever seen go-karting?'

Alys blushed. 'My parents are kind of strict.'

'Was Danny any good?' asked Naomi.

Megan nodded, her face lighting up. 'He was amazing! So fast round the track! I hardly saw him, except when he was lapping – er, overtaking – me. But I didn't do too badly in the end.' She glanced around. 'It was kind of fun.'

'What was Danny like?' asked Alys shyly. 'I mean, did he . . . *you know*.'

Megan pretended she didn't know what Alys was talking about. 'He was so nice. He said I was a really good driver.' Which wasn't *quite* true, but it might have been.

'*And*?' said Mari meaningfully.

'And what?'

'Did he . . . ?'

'Did he what?'

Mari rolled her eyes. 'Don't play dumb. Did he *kiss* you?'

The other girls fell completely silent, gazing at Megan. Megan felt hot and cold all over. 'No,' she admitted reluctantly.

There was a sigh of disappointment from her audience. 'Oh well,' said Mari, trying to sound positive, 'there's always next time.'

'He did ask me to go out with him again next weekend,' Megan said.

'Well, that's good.' Mari patted her on the back.

'He is kind of dreamy,' said Alys, a wistful look in her eyes.

'You're not the only one to think that,' said Jackie, with a curious edge to her tone.

Mari was amused. 'Maybe you should bring him along to salsa, Megan. We need some boys in this class.'

'Ooh, yes!' said Alys, a little too enthusiastically. Some of the other girls were raising their eyebrows too.

Megan shook her head. 'I don't think he'd come,' she said regretfully. 'He's not really into dancing. I think – compared to what he likes – it's a bit boring for him.'

'*Boring?*' cried Mari. 'Didn't you show him what you can do?'

'Mari, there wasn't exactly an opportunity.' Megan laughed. 'I couldn't get up on the karting track and start waltzing, could I?'

'Well, you should have,' Mari told her. 'He would be *well* impressed! You're brilliant!' The other girls nodded in agreement.

Megan felt embarrassed. 'Oh, I'm not really. It's only because I've been doing it for years.'

'You are totally amazing at it,' Jackie put in. 'Whenever I go wrong, I just look over at you to pick it up again.'

'You should be a teacher,' Mari went on. 'You're so patient with everyone.'

Alys looked around to make sure Corinne was nowhere in sight. 'And you know way more about ballroom than Corinne,' she whispered.

Mari exclaimed, 'You should teach us! Right now!' She jumped up. 'Come on! Before Corinne comes – you teach us something.'

'Ooh, yes!' Alys's eyes gleamed. 'Can you teach us a different dance? Like the foxtrot or the waltz or something?'

'No, no,' Jackie disagreed. 'I want to do Latin dances. They always look more fun on the telly. Can we do a rumba or a cha-cha?'

Megan laughed. 'You are all so funny. I can teach

you some bits if you like, but you really need a partner to do them properly.'

'Who was your partner back home?' asked one of the other girls. 'Did you have to dance with girls, like here?'

'No,' said Megan, feeling proud. 'I had a boy partner. Jake.'

'Ooh!' The other girls goggled at her. 'Wasn't it weird dancing with a boy?' asked one.

Megan laughed. 'It's not that weird. We'd been dancing together since we were really young.'

'You never told me you had a boyfriend back home!' Mari sounded injured.

'He wasn't my boyfriend,' Megan replied, getting to her feet. 'He was my dancing partner. And my friend. You know, like boy-next-door friend. I mean, he really lived next door too.'

Mari looked sceptical. 'If you say so. Guess this class must be a bit of a come-down after your old lessons then.'

Megan felt a little uncomfortable because Mari was right. 'Well, not exactly. It's just not what I'm used to, that's all.'

'OK then,' said Jackie, planting her feet firmly apart, 'I'm ready. What are you going to teach us?'

When Corinne hurried in, half an hour late, she

was astonished to find the class under way, with
Megan calling out the steps from the front. Corinne
stopped in the doorway and watched, smiling, as the
girls tried to copy Megan's kicks and flicks. But it was
only a moment or two before Megan spotted Corinne
and stopped, red with embarrassment. 'No, no,' said
Corinne, 'don't stop. That looked great! What was it
– the jive?'

'Yes,' said Megan. 'The others wanted me to show
them some steps. I thought the jive would be a good
one to start with.'

Mari was puffing with the exertion. 'It certainly
keeps you fit! Can we do some more jive, Corinne?'

Corinne smiled and put her bags down at the front
of the class. 'I'm afraid I don't know any. You'll have to
be taught by Megan.'

'That's all right,' said Mari, a little too eagerly.

Corinne laughed. 'I'm being paid to teach you,
Mari. I can't just sit by and let someone else take my
class.'

Mari bit her lip and flushed.

'But I can see you're all really getting into this,'
Corinne went on, 'so maybe we could think about
putting together a routine. You could practise in the
last few minutes of each lesson.'

Mari brightened up. 'That sounds fab! Could we

do a performance somewhere?' This announcement was met by noises of horror from the other girls. Mari looked crestfallen. 'Only a suggestion.'

'I don't think you're quite there yet.' Corinne smiled at her. 'But you never know, if you work hard. Right, back to the new steps we were practising last week.'

Megan meekly took her place in the class again, but inside she was buzzing. She'd never tried to teach a whole class before. She couldn't believe how much she'd enjoyed it! And the girls were so enthusiastic and supportive!

She looked around warmly at the other girls. She was starting to feel as though she had real friends again. Especially Mari – she was such fun to be around.

And then there was always Danny . . . her heart skipped a beat as she thought of him.

Maybe moving to Parchester had been a good idea after all?

Chapter 9

I think you're really cool

Samantha examined a nail. 'You wouldn't catch *me* wearing that,' she commented, nodding towards the start line, where Danny and Paul were lined up with a crowd of others on BMX bikes. Both of them were fully kitted out with knee and elbow pads, plus helmets with visors.

'Me neither,' echoed Jasmine.

Megan wondered what on earth the two of them were doing here. When Danny had invited her along, she had thought it would be some kind of friends get-together thing, where everyone had a bit of a go on the bikes and they had some silly races. But this was serious. There were marshals organizing the groups on their bikes, and even a St John's Ambulance crew on standby in case of accidents. The three girls were standing on the edge of a muddy track, and while Megan had dressed in an unattractive yet warm anorak, Jasmine and Samantha were attired in matching denim jackets. Both of them were shivering and they'd only arrived half an hour ago.

Megan wasn't sure whether to feel amused or exasperated. 'I didn't realize it would be quite like this,' she muttered.

Samantha gave a snort. 'Thought you'd be having a nice cosy one-to-one on a bike?'

'No, of course not. But I didn't realize it was such a big deal.' She looked curiously at Samantha. 'Do you *like* coming to these things?'

Jasmine laughed and then tried to turn it into a cough. Samantha glared at her. 'Not much else to do, is there?' she said carelessly. 'Saturday afternoons are so boring in Parchester.'

'You could go – I don't know – shopping, or something,' suggested Megan.

'Got no money,' said Samantha flatly.

Megan was surprised. Samantha always looked so neatly turned out, with her polished nails and her sleek hair. 'Oh. I thought . . . well, never mind.'

'She had her allowance docked,' Jasmine whispered when Samantha was looking the other way. 'After what happened in the summer.' She narrowed her eyes. 'There was this thing she did when she was in a play . . .'

'Yes.' Megan was uncomfortable. 'Yes, I heard.'

'Most people stopped talking to her after that,' Jasmine went on confidentially. 'She used to be really popular. She had a friend called Eloise but she went off with someone else.'

'She didn't go off with someone else,' said Samantha coldly. Jasmine gulped. 'I told her she was a useless piece of debris and I didn't want to see her again.'

'Right.' Megan shook her head in disbelief. The way Samantha behaved – it was so *rude*. How could she treat people like that? 'Are you – were you sorry? About what happened, I mean?' The moment the words were out of her mouth, she knew it was completely the wrong thing to say.

Samantha's gaze turned as icy as the wind. 'I don't know what you're talking about.' She turned her back on Megan.

Megan glanced at Jasmine, who shrugged. Megan wanted to say, 'But if you know she's so awful, why do you hang out with her?' And then Jasmine glanced over at the boys waiting to start the race, and Megan knew the answer. *Danny.* As if he knew Megan was looking at him he lifted his visor and waved, grinning. She waved back, and then he snapped his visor down again and the gun went to start the race.

Megan had never realized before just how much skill was needed to navigate a BMX track. Her jaw dropped as she saw the group charge towards the first set of small hillocks and almost bounce from one to the next. Several fell, but Danny flew over them as if they were merely bumps in the road. As the group rounded the first corner, Danny was already pulling away from the majority. Megan clenched her fists without even noticing. She couldn't take her eyes off him. Every hole in the track; every hump – Megan felt her heart thud in case he fell off. Beside her, Jasmine too was standing riveted to the spot, her gaze never leaving Danny's figure.

When he crossed the finishing line first, Megan burst out cheering. 'That was amazing!'

Jasmine was nodding as though her head would fall off, but she hadn't uttered a sound. Her almond-shaped eyes blazed with intensity.

Danny punched the air, and then pulled off his helmet. His dark spiky hair was a mess of tangles, and his cheeks were flushed. He slapped hands with Paul, who had come in an unimpressive seventh, and then glanced over towards the girls. Megan caught her breath. He radiated energy. You could almost feel it pouring out of him, even at this distance. And now he was coming over . . .

'What did you think?'

Megan threw her arms around him, heedless of the

mud spatters. Behind her, Samantha made a noise of disgust. 'You were *brilliant*!'

Danny hugged her back. 'Thanks! It was a great race. I didn't think I was going to take that guy in front of me to start with.'

'But you did!' Megan pulled back, suddenly embarrassed. She had hugged him in front of everyone! But he didn't seem to mind . . . She started talking again to hide her confusion. 'I can't believe you didn't fall off. How do you even cycle on ground like that?'

'Do you want a go?' asked Danny. 'I can show you.'

Megan hesitated. She *did* want a go. It looked mad and crazy, and a bit dangerous – and she really wanted to try it. She opened her mouth to say, 'YES', but all of a sudden she was very aware of Jasmine standing next to her. Jasmine seemed to have shrunk in some way. Her dark curtain of hair had fallen back across her face, and she was examining the ground. Megan felt a wave of something like pity. Why was Jasmine so shy all the time? If she hung out with Samantha so often, surely she wanted to be part of things? On an impulse, she said, 'Why don't you show *both* of us? Jasmine and me. I bet she'd like a go too.'

Jasmine's head snapped up in alarm. 'Oh no,' she

said, stuttering a little. 'I don't think . . . I mean, I wouldn't be any good . . .'

Megan grabbed her hand. Jasmine's fingers were freezing. 'You'll be fine,' she said firmly. 'What do you think, Danny?'

Danny looked taken aback. 'Uh . . . yeah, I guess. If you say so.'

'Cool,' Megan said.

Danny grinned. 'You want a go too, Sam?'

Samantha made a noise that sounded like, 'Tchuh!' Paul, who had been bringing up the rear as usual, looked disappointed. 'Come on, Sam,' he said encouragingly. 'If the others are having a go, you might find you like it.'

Samantha gave him a withering look. 'As *if*,' she said. 'I wouldn't get on that thing for a million pounds.'

'I thought you had no money?' Megan said before she could stop herself.

Danny shouted with laughter. 'Gotcha there, sis. Come on, don't be a spoilsport.'

Samantha, two pink spots glowing on her cheeks, glared at him. 'I am *not*,' she said clearly, 'getting on a bike.' She cast a look at Paul. 'I'm *hungry*.'

He jumped into action. 'I'll get you something to eat. You want a burger?'

'Come on,' Danny said to Megan. 'We'll go find somewhere quieter.'

Megan dragged Jasmine along beside her. Danny led them to a section of field that was less crowded than the rest. It was still very muddy though, and Megan wished she'd worn wellies instead of trainers. 'Hold this,' Danny jerked the bike towards Megan and started to take off his elbow and knee pads.

'I think Jasmine should go first,' said Megan.

Danny threw her an odd look. 'If you say so.'

Jasmine was still protesting. 'I don't think this is really . . . oh, do you think they'll fit? My head is kind of small, you know . . . I don't think this helmet is . . . how do you see out of it?'

Megan felt mildly irritated. Couldn't Jasmine just get on with it?

Danny snapped the visor shut and Jasmine squeaked. He glanced at Megan. 'Why did you want her to have a go? She's going to be useless.'

'She hasn't even tried yet,' Megan pointed out.

'I can still hear you, you know,' said Jasmine in a small voice.

Danny sighed. 'All right. Get on the bike.' He started to show her the gears and the brakes, and how to balance on the pedals. Megan could tell Jasmine was hanging on his every word, but she was so nervous she kept forgetting what he told her. 'No!' Danny snapped in exasperation. 'Push *back* on the right foot, and *forward* on the left foot. Are you deaf or some-thing?'

'Sorry,' said Jasmine miserably, wobbling so hard she nearly fell off. She sounded close to tears. 'I'm trying.'

Megan knew she should feel sorry for Jasmine, but it was exasperating how *wet* the girl was being! Didn't she have any backbone at all? Watching her wobble around was so frustrating! Megan was becoming impatient to try it out herself. 'Shall I have a go now?' she offered. 'Then maybe Jasmine could have another try later.' She wished she hadn't bothered involving Jasmine.

Jasmine got off the bike. 'Yeah, maybe,' she said in a muffled voice.

'No way,' said Danny decidedly. 'She'll break my bike if she's not careful. And I'm signed up for another race later.'

Jasmine held out the helmet to Megan, shaking her hair into her face as usual. 'There you go.'

'I thought you did really well,' Megan lied, but she was taken aback by the venomous look Jasmine gave her.

'No you didn't,' Jasmine muttered. 'You just wanted me to go first so I'd make you look good.'

Megan's mouth fell open. 'What?' She couldn't believe what she was hearing! And after she had made an extra effort to involve Jasmine, too!

'Come on, come on,' said Danny impatiently.

Megan hastily pulled on the helmet, remembering to pull her hairband out this time. She didn't want another headache from her ponytail. Jasmine turned away. Megan ignored her. If Jasmine wanted to sulk, she could do it on her own.

'You have ridden a bike before, right?'

'Of course I have,' said Megan, offended.

'Well, this isn't like riding any ordinary bike,' said Danny. 'I'll talk you through it.' He was soon lost in explaining the balance and steering. Megan listened closely and tried to follow his instructions. 'That's good,' he told her. 'Keep your knees flexible.'

'Can I try going over some of those hump things?'

Danny grinned. 'You're keen. I think there's a practice track round the other side of the field. You want to go over and see it?'

'Yeah!' Megan said enthusiastically. 'Oh. Hang on.' She looked around. 'Where's Jasmine?'

Danny shrugged. 'Dunno. Why?'

Megan hesitated. She knew that she ought to go

after Jasmine; make sure she was all right. Jasmine had no one else to hang around with, and Samantha and Paul had disappeared off to the burger vans. But something in Megan rebelled. Why should *she* be the one to look after Jasmine? Especially as Jasmine had just been rude to her. If Jasmine didn't like it here, she could just go home, couldn't she?

Megan made up her mind. 'Oh, no reason. Come on then, let's go to the practice track.'

As they walked over, Danny commented, 'You should be wearing proper kit if you're going to ride, but I guess it'll be OK.'

'Proper kit?'

'Yeah. Protection. Leathers.' He glanced sideways. 'If you're going to come regularly we should get you some. Jeans won't last long if you fall.'

'Oh, right.' Megan felt a sudden qualm. For a moment she had completely forgotten about the risk of injury. *Maybe I'm becoming more of a daredevil?* she wondered to herself. For some reason, the thought made her feel quite excited.

Danny was holding out a hand. 'You see these gloves? They're extra tough. You have to practically stab them with a carving knife to make a dent.'

'Wow. They look kind of expensive.'

He nodded. 'They are. And the trousers are about a

million times more expensive. I only got them because they were second hand. Even then I had to use my modelling money.' He glanced sideways at Megan. 'I do modelling for catalogues.' His voice sounded both proud and slightly self-conscious.

'Yeah, someone at dance told me,' Megan replied.

Danny looked a bit put out that this news wasn't a surprise.

She went on hastily. 'It sounds really cool.'

He shrugged. 'It's all right. A lot of standing around most of the time. But the money is good, and it means I can buy stuff for my skateboard.'

Megan looked down at the handlebars. 'What about this bike?'

Danny shrugged. 'Oh, that's one of Paul's old bikes. He gave it to me.'

'He *gave* it to you?' Megan stared. 'Aren't they expensive too?'

'Yeah, but Paul's rolling in it.' Danny grinned suddenly. 'It's probably why Samantha's going out with him.'

Megan wrinkled her nose. 'For his money?'

'Yeah.' Danny laughed. 'Well, she hasn't got any of her own, has she? Not since she lost dear Daddy's approval.' He laughed again.

Megan felt a bit surprised that Danny didn't seem

to feel sorry for Samantha at all. But then Samantha had got into a lot of trouble, hadn't she? Maybe
Danny was still angry with her about that. It made her
curious to know more about him. He didn't really act
like a supportive big brother to her. Megan couldn't
imagine being that mean about Owen, no matter how
annoying he was being.

The practice track was swarming with eager young-
sters trying their skills. 'It looks a bit crowded,' said
Megan doubtfully.

'There's always space for one more,' Danny said.
'You just have to act confident.'

Megan got on the bike and took a breath.

'Now, remember what I told you.'

She nodded. 'I got it.' And then she was off! This
was crazier than driving a go-kart! Every bump, every
jolt sent shudders through her. The saddle was no
protection, but Danny kept yelling, 'Stay up on the
pedals!' and then suddenly she hit her stride and flew
over a hump, landing with a thump but managing
to stay upright. Megan grinned and gripped the
handlebars even tighter. This was mad! Crazy!
Wild! She loved it!

It wasn't until she heard Danny yelling that Megan
realized she'd been round the practice track five times
already. Suddenly embarrassed, she pulled off the

track and rode over. 'Sorry!' she said breathlessly. 'I forgot what I was doing.'

Danny grinned. 'Looks to me like you had it figured out just fine. You're a natural.'

'Really?' Megan pulled off her helmet and scraped her hair back from her flushed cheeks. 'It does seem to come quite easily. I mean, nothing like you. But I thought I was better than some of the other people practising.'

'Way better,' said Danny appreciatively. 'But I had to call you over because I need the bike back. My next race is coming up.'

'Oh no, I'm so sorry!'

He laughed. 'It's fine. I'm not late or anything.' His expression suddenly sobered. 'You look amazing.'

Megan didn't know what to say. 'Oh. Thanks.'

'I liked it earlier,' he said suddenly, 'when you ran over to me. After the race.'

'Oh.' Megan blushed.

'I think you're really cool,' said Danny.

'Really?' Megan felt hot and cold all over.

He nodded. 'Really.' And then he leaned forward and kissed her. Right on the lips. Right in front of everyone. It wasn't a long kiss, but Megan felt for a moment as though her feet had lost their grip on the ground.

The loudhailer blared, and Danny's head jerked back. 'That's my race.' He grabbed his helmet and turned his bike round. 'See you in a bit.'

Megan didn't even have a chance to call 'Good luck!' after him. She stood, slightly dazed, wondering if anyone had noticed what had just happened. The nearest people seemed totally uninterested in Megan. She couldn't see Samantha or Paul. She breathed out. Nobody had noticed. She wasn't sure if she was pleased or disappointed. The most momentous event in her life so far – her first kiss! – and no one had seen it!

No, that wasn't quite true. There was one person looking, though she was at a distance, and Megan only recognized her from the dark curtain of hair that fell across the blazing stare. If Jasmine had disliked Megan before, she certainly hated her now.

Chapter 10

how do you know you fancy him?

'He kissed you!' Mari cried, bouncing up and down on Megan's bed. 'I can't believe it! That is so cool!'

'Now you see why I couldn't tell you over the phone?' asked Megan.

'Of course! Anyway, I was running out of credit so we couldn't have talked about it properly,' said Mari. 'Though I can't stay long today. Victoria's going to this posh do and she's asked me to go with her.'

'What kind of posh do?' asked Megan, interested. Mari mentioned Victoria and Fliss quite a lot but she never seemed to go into very much detail about them.

'Oh, I don't know,' said Mari in a dismissive tone. 'Some opening of an art gallery or something. Her parents have put up the money, I think.' She saw Megan's face. 'I know. Victoria's got oodles of money. Her parents are always out working. She's got an au pair too.'

'A what?'

'You know, a sort of live-in home-help babysitter.' Mari flapped her hand helplessly. 'It's kind of weird that Victoria and I are friends because our families are *sooo* different. My mother would *kill* for an au pair, but we'd only be able to pay her about twenty pence a week. I hate having no money. It's a good thing the salsa class is cheap.'

Megan felt even more glad that she had lent Mari her silver shoes.

'Anyway, anyway,' Mari went on, 'tell me *everything*. What was it like? Kissing Danny, I mean?'

'Well,' said Megan, feeling a smile spread across her face, 'it was . . . it was really nice.'

Mari stared at her. 'Nice? Just nice?'

'Um . . .' Megan's smile faltered. Now that she came to think about it again, she wasn't sure she could remember *exactly* how it had felt. She closed her eyes for a moment. There he was, leaning towards her . . . and she leaned towards him . . . and . . . Megan's eyes opened. 'I can't really remember.'

Mari looked disappointed. 'Oh.'

'Do you think that's bad?' Megan was worried. 'I mean, I should be able to, shouldn't I?'

Mari shrugged. 'I dunno. I'm not an expert. I've

only kissed Sean a couple of times and they were both kind of by accident.'

'It's just that . . .' Megan began, before Mari's words filtered through her brain. 'You what? Mari – have you got a *boyfriend*?'

'Oh yes,' said Mari carelessly. 'Didn't I mention him?'

'You certainly did not!' Megan spluttered. She couldn't believe she'd known Mari for weeks and Mari had never even spoken about it before! 'But . . . what . . . who . . . what's he like?'

Mari leaned back against the wall and stared at the ceiling light. 'His name's Sean. He's tall and he's got red hair.'

Megan waited expectantly. 'And?'

Mari shrugged. 'And what? He's all right. Not particularly good-looking.'

Megan felt baffled. 'You sound as though you don't like him much.'

'I do,' said Mari instantly. 'Well – I think I do.' She sighed. 'Oh, what's the big deal anyway? He's nice. He's funny. We have a laugh. Why does it have to be this massive BOYFRIEND thing?'

Megan stared. 'I don't know. But I sort of thought you'd fancy him if you were going out with him.' Mari wrinkled her nose. '*Do* you fancy him?'

For the first time, Mari looked embarrassed. 'I don't know. Sometimes I think I do, sometimes I don't.'

Megan didn't know what to say. 'How does he feel about you?'

'Oh, he fancies me,' said Mari airily. 'He tells me all the time.'

'Maybe he's hoping you'll say it back.'

'But I'm not sure,' said Mari, chewing her lip. 'How can I say it if I'm not sure?'

There was silence for a few minutes. 'Maybe you'll sort of come to fancy him over time,' said Megan lamely.

'We've been going out since the end of August,' said Mari. 'Wouldn't I know by now?'

Megan bit her lip. 'I don't know.'

'You fancy Danny, don't you?'

'Well – yes.'

'So how does it feel?' Mari leaned forward. 'I mean, when you see him, how do you feel? How do you *know* you fancy him?'

Now it was Megan's turn to feel embarrassed. 'Well, I – er . . . I sort of get this funny feeling in my stomach. Like it's buzzing or wriggling or something. It makes me feel a little bit sick.'

Mari screwed up her nose. 'Sounds horrible.'

'Not exactly – it's kind of weird and exciting at the

same time. Like – um – like when you have to stand up in Assembly and say something, or when you're in a play. Like nerves, I guess.'

'Oh!' Mari's expression cleared. 'I get you. Like stage fright.'

'Yes, sort of. And then when he smiles at me . . .' Megan thought for a moment. 'It's sort of like I keep noticing how good-looking he is. And it makes me feel warm because he's smiling at *me*, not at anyone else. And so that makes me more nervous to do everything right, because I want him to keep smiling at me. So I'm always really aware of everything I do.'

'Sounds exhausting,' Mari commented. 'Can't you just – you know – be yourself around him? I mean, like we're talking now?'

Megan laughed. 'Of course not! I can't relax at all when he's around! It's like being next to a really hot fire; bright and exciting but you don't want to get burned. And besides, I can't talk about the stuff I like – dancing and that. Because he's not really interested.'

Mari was shaking her head doubtfully. 'Doesn't sound like that much fun to me.'

'But I get to do all this new exciting stuff!' replied Megan. Why couldn't Mari see? 'Skateboarding and go-karting and BMX riding – I've never done any of that before. It's like a whole new world.'

'I feel a song coming on,' said Mari dryly.

Megan felt frustrated. 'But it is. And it's really exciting – and he shows me how to do it, and it's *fun.*'

'Dancing is fun.'

'Yes it is, and I love it, but . . .'

'You should make him do something *you* like,' went on Mari, her voice becoming stronger. 'I mean, I know me and Sean aren't perfect, but I don't let him choose what we're going to do all the time. If there's something I want to go to – a concert, say – then he comes with me. Even if it's not something he'd have chosen. That's what you do.'

Megan felt a little bewildered. Hadn't they just been talking about how important it was to fancy someone if you were going out with them? And here was Mari now saying it was more important to share interests. 'Maybe I will,' she said defensively.

'You should. I know!' Mari's face lit up. '*Riverdance* is coming to the Parchester Apollo Theatre. You should take him. Then he'll see the sort of thing you like, and maybe he'll like it too.'

'I'm not sure . . .' Megan began, but Mari interrupted.

'Look, Megan, do you know how he feels about you?'

'Not exactly . . .'

'Then this is a good way to find out, isn't it? Because if he comes to *Riverdance* with you and is prepared to give it a go, then he obviously wants to make you happy, doesn't he? And *that's* how you can tell if he fancies you.'

♥

Megan was bursting to tell Jake all about the BMX meet, but he sounded a bit tired. 'Are you OK?'

'Yeah, sorry. I just – there's lots of stuff going on here, Meg. My stepdad's been made redundant.'

'What? Oh no, that's awful!' Jake's stepdad Stephen was an architect, like Megan's dad. Only he mainly designed residential homes rather than office build-ings like Bryan. 'When did that happen?'

'Three days ago.' Jake sighed. 'Turns out they'd been threatening to do it for ages, but he didn't tell Mum because he didn't want her to worry.'

'Why did he lose his job? Did he – did he do some-thing wrong?'

'No,' Jake replied. 'No, it's just that fewer people are having their homes designed by architects these days.

Fewer people are having extensions built. You know, there's just less work around because people haven't got much money right now. So the firm decided they'd have to let someone go, and since Stephen was the last one in, he was the first one out. He's gutted.'

'I'm so sorry.' Megan thought about Jake's stepdad and how much fun he was to be around. 'Can he get another job?'

Jake made a noise that sounded like a half-snort, half-laugh. 'Where? There aren't many jobs for architects, as you know. Your dad was lucky to get his.'

'Lucky we had to move two hundred miles away?' protested Megan.

'At least he's *got* a job. Mum says the redundancy money won't last three months. After that – well . . .' Jake gulped. 'Mum says she could go back to being a classroom assistant. But that doesn't pay so well.'

'I'm so sorry,' said Megan again, feeling useless. 'Maybe things will work out OK?'

'Yeah, maybe,' said Jake. 'And maybe not.'

'I wish there was something I could do,' said Megan wistfully.

'Yeah, me too. Listen, Meg, I've got to go. I'll talk to you soon, OK?'

Megan felt ashamed when she hung up. She had been so wrapped up in her own life, she had hardly bothered to get in touch with Jake recently. Stephen had lost his job three days ago – why hadn't Jake rung to tell her? *But then*, she thought, *I haven't rung him for a whole week either. I've been too preoccupied with my new friends. When I should have been more concerned about my old one.*

♥

Megan's mind wasn't really on dancing at the next salsa class. She did the steps almost automatically whilst worrying about Jake. She wished there was something she could do to help, but she was two hundred miles away now – what could she possibly do?

'Good work, Mari,' came Corinne's voice. 'That's so much better than last week.'

Mari beamed and turned to Megan. 'Did you hear that?'

'What?'

'Earth to Megan.' Mari waved a hand in front of her face. 'Everything OK?'

'Hmm? Oh – yeah. Just had some bad news from Jake the other evening. His stepdad lost his job.'

'Oh.' Mari looked sympathetic. 'Sorry.'

'I'm just a bit down at the moment, that's all,' Megan said, attempting a smile.

'Did you book tickets for *Riverdance*, like I suggested?'

'Yeah, that's all done. I told Danny we're going to the theatre but he doesn't know what we're going to see.'

'Excellent.' Mari patted her on the arm. 'Cheer up, then. It's not all that bad.'

Megan smiled but it made her face ache. It wasn't just Jake's news that was depressing her, she knew. She was missing her dancing desperately. Nice though the other girls were, the salsa class just wasn't up to her standard. She missed the other dance styles too – the precision of the quickstep; the carnival feel of the samba. Megan was beginning to worry that if she didn't find a more advanced class soon, she'd forget all her skills. And what if she *never* found one here in Parchester . . . ? She missed dancing with a good partner most of all. When they paired up in this class, Megan invariably found herself dancing with Mari, who would be the first to admit she was a complete beginner. Megan longed for a partner who could match her in skill. She missed Jake so much!

'Come and sit down, everyone,' Corinne called. 'I know it's not yet seven, but I've got some things to discuss with you.'

The girls gathered on the floor.

'Now, I've got two ideas to run by you,' Corinne went on. 'The first one is this.' She held up a colourful flyer. 'It's for the Ace of Hearts restaurant in Parchester. They're holding a salsa evening at the beginning of November. You get dinner and dancing included in the price. I wondered if you'd all like to go, as a sort of group outing?'

Excited chatter broke out. 'That sounds fab,' said Jackie, her eyes shining.

'As long as we don't have to do some kind of performance,' Alys put in pointedly.

Corinne laughed. 'No, absolutely not. This is a fun evening out. I didn't know anything about it until my friend Candy passed this flyer to me.'

'I'm in,' said Mari decidedly. 'If there's dinner included, I'm there.' She grinned at Megan, who tried to smile back.

'Excellent,' said Corinne. 'You all need to check with your parents that you're allowed to go. You'll need to be dropped off and picked up from the Ace of Hearts. And you'll need money to pay for the dinner. I'll book us a table, but please let me know if you can't come.' She put the flyer down. 'Now, the other idea.' She glanced at Megan and took a breath. 'I've been thinking about giving Megan a bit to do in the class – you know, teaching you guys some different dances, like we discussed.'

Mari grinned at Megan, whose face was turning pink.

'And I wondered,' Corinne continued, 'whether you'd like some kind of end-of-term Christmas party. A dancing party, of course. With family and friends. And Megan could teach you the jive – properly, so you could do a short routine to show people. Along with some salsa, of course.'

The chatter erupted into full-blown excitement. 'A party!' shouted Jackie.

'With fairy lights!' called someone else. 'And a Christmas tree!'

'And sparkly costumes,' suggested Alys.

'I would *love* to learn the jive,' said Mari, her eyes shining. 'The bit we did the other day was so much fun!' The other girls agreed.

Megan almost felt like bursting into tears with gratitude. The girls all thought it was a fantastic idea that she should teach them the jive! How lovely of them! It wouldn't be the same as finding a new class or dancing with Jake, of course, but if she were allowed to choreograph a whole routine . . . what an opportunity!

'What do you think, Megan?' asked Corinne, who had been watching her. 'Would you be up for that?'

Megan smiled from ear to ear. 'Definitely!'

'Woo-hoo!' cried Mari. 'I love parties! Ooh!' Her face suddenly changed. 'You could invite Danny.'

'Ooh yes,' said Jackie eagerly.

'Not Samantha though,' added Mari, frowning. 'Just Danny.'

Megan laughed. 'I don't think it would be his kind of thing. But I could ask him, I guess.' *And then he could see what I love doing best*, she thought with a glow. *And maybe he'll understand, like I understand his passion for racing.* She suddenly felt a lot better. *And I'm taking Danny to* Riverdance *at the weekend*, she remembered. *I can talk to him much more about dancing then.*

'Good,' said Corinne, getting up. 'We'll talk about music and routines next week. I'll look into hiring the community hall or something. Don't forget to ask your parents about the dinner at the Ace of Hearts. Take a flyer each so you've got all the details.'

Mari swung round to Megan. 'This is going to be so brilliant! And if you bring Danny . . .' She waggled her eyebrows up and down.

Megan laughed. 'We'll see. I think the only way he'd agree to come was if we were performing the jive on rollerskates.'

The girls bundled out of the arts centre, chatting

and laughing excitedly. 'Can't wait for the jive,' Alys said as she waved goodbye to Megan.

'Me too,' agreed Jackie. 'Such a cool dance! I bet Megan will come up with something really amazing.'

Megan felt a rush of affection for them all. She smiled and waved goodbye in return.

'Glad you've cheered up,' said Mari, nudging her. 'You looked really down when we arrived.'

'I was,' said Megan. 'But I'm really excited about choreographing a dance. I love that kind of thing. Jake and I used to choreograph our own routines sometimes too.'

'You should ask him to come to the party,' said Mari.

Megan shook her head. 'He lives two hundred miles away, Mari. And it'll still be term time.'

'You could ask him,' persisted Mari.

'Well, maybe. You should ask Fliss and Victoria.'

Mari's face lit up. 'That's such a good idea! I will, you know. Not sure if Fliss will be doing her filming thing, but I should be able to drag Victoria along.' She frowned suddenly. 'But you *are* going to ask Jake to come visit sometime, aren't you? I want to meet him.'

'He's meant to be coming down in half-term,' Megan told her.

Mari gave a whoop. 'Perfect! Can't wait to meet him

– and you have to dance with him. I bet the two of you are just amazing. You could do the jive – we could get the girls together!'

Megan laughed. 'The jive isn't our strongest dance. The waltz is our favourite. We won a competition with that one.'

'The waltz then,' said Mari. 'Sounds dreamy. We'll tell the girls and we can all meet up, since salsa won't be on during half-term.'

Megan felt a little alarmed. 'Jake's not coming down to give a performance, Mari. He's just coming for a visit.'

'I know,' said Mari, 'but there's no harm in asking, is there?'

Chapter 11

you look cute when you laugh

Danny's jaw dropped. '*How* much? For a *programme?*'

Megan felt anxious. 'Don't worry. I'll get it.' She fumbled with her purse.

'Do you really need one?'

'I like looking at the pictures,' Megan replied, and then realized how lame that sounded. 'I sometimes cut them out and put them on my wall.' Even worse!

Danny was staring at the posters. 'I didn't know we were coming to watch a dance show. It's not really my kind of thing.'

Megan put on an encouraging expression. 'But it's good to try new stuff, isn't it? You might like it, you never know.'

Danny didn't look so sure.

As soon as they took their seats in the theatre, Megan knew this date wasn't going to be a success.

Danny complained that the seat wasn't comfortable and that there wasn't enough leg-room. When the overture started, he was still looking around and whispering. An irritated woman on the other side of him told him to be quiet. Danny made a face at Megan, but she felt so embarrassed she pretended she hadn't heard anything.

Megan loved the music of *Riverdance*. She had listened to the soundtrack over and over again at home. It was so evocative; she could almost imagine Irish faeries emerging from the auditorium. And when the curtain rose, she sat forward in anticipation. She had seen snippets of the show on television, but never in a live theatre. The dancing enthralled her. She marvelled at their skill – fancy being able to leap so high whilst your arms were held down by your sides! And the flamenco and tap routines were so complicated, too!

Danny fidgeted. Megan wanted to concentrate on the stage, but he shifted his position first one way, then the other. Then he started to sigh – not loudly, but enough to distract her. 'Is anything the matter?' she whispered.

'My legs are going to sleep,' he whispered back. 'When's the interval?'

'Not for ages yet.'

He sighed again.

Megan really wanted to enjoy the first half. The show was fascinating. There was so much to see! She felt she could watch the show twenty times and still not notice everything that was happening onstage. But all the way through she was aware of Danny fussing and fidgeting. She was almost relieved when it was time for the interval.

Danny stood up immediately. 'My feet have pins and needles!' he said, hopping from one foot to the other. The woman on his other side gave him a poisonous look.

'We could go and get some ice cream,' suggested Megan, hoping that the five pounds left in her purse would cover it. 'They're selling them down by the stage.'

'Can't we get some fresh air?' asked Danny.

'If you like.'

They picked up their coats and made their way to the exit. It was a slow business because the theatre was packed.

'Whew!' said Danny as they emerged into the street. 'That's better!' He turned and grinned at Megan. 'It was hot in there!'

She smiled back. 'I know you're an outdoorsy kind of person.'

'Totally. Hate being cramped up like that.'

'The show's good though, isn't it?' asked Megan hopefully.

Danny shrugged. 'It's all right, I suppose. If you like that kind of thing. Could do with more action though. It's a bit boring in places. And that woman who comes on and sings warbly songs is starting to do my head in.'

Megan hadn't thought that a single second was boring, but she kept quiet. She was disappointed he hadn't liked it more though. 'Didn't you think those men were amazing? They must have legs made out of muscle!'

'It's just a lot of jumping around,' said Danny dismissively. 'And then they get a new costume and do it all again.'

'But they're using all sorts of different styles of dance,' said Megan, starting to feel slightly irritated. 'It's not the same kind of thing all the time.'

Danny rolled his eyes. 'Jumping up and down, prancing around a bit. It all looks the same to me.'

Megan bit her lip. Maybe this had been a bad idea, expecting Danny to like a dance show. Maybe she should have taken him to a musical instead . . . or a concert? 'Never mind,' she said persuasively, 'the second half is shorter.' She shivered in the cold air.

'Let's go and get in the queue for ice cream before we have to go back to our seats.'

'I've got a better idea,' said Danny. 'Why don't we go to the ice-cream place down the road?'

Megan stared. 'We haven't got time. We'll miss the second half.'

'That's the plan. Come on!' Danny grabbed her hand, but Megan pulled away.

'I want to see the second half.' He surely didn't mean it?

'I can do it for you.' Danny jumped up and down a bit, kicking up his feet in a ridiculous way. 'There, you see? Come on, let's go and get warm.'

'I've been looking forward to this.' Megan felt tears prick at her eyes. She knew the soundtrack inside out; it would be too unfair to miss half the show! 'And I bought the tickets.'

Danny paused for a moment and looked at her more closely. Then he unexpectedly put his arms around her. 'Don't be sad,' he said softly in her ear. 'You can see it another time, can't you? It's just that my legs are killing me. I don't think I can spend another hour in those seats. And the woman next to me hates me too. I'll just get on everyone's nerves.'

Megan resisted. 'You could put up with it for my sake.'

Danny sighed and let go of her. 'You go back in then. I'll meet you down the road after it's finished.'

'What?' Megan stared.

'I can't sit through any more,' said Danny in a pleading tone. 'I'm really sorry, Megan. I'll go and get some ice cream and wait for you.'

'But . . .'

The bell rang, signalling the imminent start of the second half. Megan felt torn. She really wanted to see the rest of the show. But they were on a *date*; she couldn't just let Danny go off on his own, could she? It wasn't his fault he didn't like dancing; it was her fault for asking him along to something she should have known he wouldn't like.

Danny put a gentle hand under Megan's chin and tilted it up. 'Come and get ice cream with me,' he said in a coaxing voice. 'You can have whatever you want. Honeycomb? Coffee and walnut? Blueberry sorbet? They've got it all, you know.'

Megan pulled a rueful face and gave in. 'Oh, all right. I suppose I can't force you into that seat.'

'That's my girl.' Danny put an arm around her shoulders and they walked away from the theatre.

Megan ignored the tiny sorrowful protest inside her.

♥

'So,' said Danny, once they had their chocolate brown-ies and ice cream in front of them, 'you ever done any modelling?'

'Me?' Megan was startled. 'No, never.'

'I think you should.' Danny dug into his brownie with gusto. 'They love red-heads. And you've got good bone structure.'

Megan laughed. 'What do you know about bone structure?'

'They told me about it at the agency,' Danny said complacently. 'They looked at my photos when I first went in with Samantha.' He grinned. 'They said I had better bone structure than her. She was really mad.'

Megan still felt disappointed about the show, but she tried to sound interested. 'Have you done a lot of modelling?'

'More than Samantha. There are more girl models than boys so I get more work.'

'I wouldn't have thought . . .' Megan stopped. She didn't want to offend Danny. 'I'm surprised you like doing it, I mean.'

'You get paid to wear stuff and just stand around,' he said. 'What's not to like?'

'Does it pay well?'

'Yeah, mostly. Mum and Dad only let me have half though. They put the rest into a bank account.'

'And you think I could be a model?' Megan was thawing a little. 'Am I pretty enough?'

'It's not just about being pretty,' Danny said. 'It's about charisma. You know, when people can't take their eyes off you. You've got something that makes people go "wow!"'

Megan raised her eyebrows. 'Have I got that?'

'Oh yeah, definitely.' He grinned again. 'Why do you think I'm hanging out with you?'

Megan felt a warm glow. She could forgive him for making her miss the second half of the show if he said things like that! He couldn't take his eyes off her! He must fancy her, then, if he felt that way . . . 'I really like you,' she said impulsively, and then bit her lip. She hadn't meant to say that out loud!

'Yeah, me too,' said Danny, cutting chunks off his brownie with the side of his fork.

Megan blinked. That wasn't quite the reaction she had expected. Should she say more? 'I love spending time with you,' she said. 'And I love trying out new stuff. You know, like the go-karts and the bikes the other day . . . it was amazing! I never thought

I'd like doing things like that. I've spent most of my free time dancing, since I was little.'

'You should try rollerblading,' Danny said. 'You'd love it.'

Megan felt a bit frustrated. Couldn't he see what she was trying to say? 'What I mean is,' she said carefully, 'I *really* like you. You know?'

'Yeah. I really like you too.' He grinned. 'Are you going to finish yours?'

'Huh?' Megan stared. Danny gestured towards her plate. 'Oh. No – you have it.'

'Cheers.'

Out of nowhere, Megan felt an irresistible urge to laugh. Were all boys this dense? Here she was, trying to pour her heart and her feelings out to Danny, and he . . . well, he was still thinking about ice cream! She couldn't help it. She giggled.

Danny looked up. 'What? Have I got ice cream on my chin or something?'

'No.' Megan flapped her hand. 'No, it's nothing.' This was so ridiculous!

'This is good ice cream,' said Danny.

Megan giggled even louder. 'Sorry,' she gasped. 'I don't even know why I'm laughing!'

Danny smiled. 'You look cute when you laugh.'

That just made Megan laugh even more. He thought

she looked cute when she was angry, sad, laughing
. . . and yet he didn't notice when she tried to tell him
how much she fancied him! She had to get a grip.
Think about something else. Think about dancing. Oh –
the Christmas party! 'D'you want to come to a party?
Middle of December.'

Danny looked interested. 'Yeah, why not? Who's
having a party?'

'My salsa class. We're going to hire a hall or something and have a proper party, with fairy lights and a
Christmas tree and everything.'

'Oh.' Danny didn't look so impressed. '*That* kind
of party.'

'And dancing,' Megan went on. 'You could
come and see what I do. What I'm good at. It's
not like *Riverdance*,' she added hastily, seeing his
expression. 'It's proper ballroom dancing. They've
even asked me to choreograph a jive for the whole
class!'

Danny raised his eyebrows. 'Is that good?'

'It's brilliant!' Megan beamed. 'The jive is such a
cool dance. Will you come?'

Danny looked uncertain. 'Dunno. It's not really my
kind of thing.'

Megan's face fell. 'Oh. Well, see what you think nearer
the time. It's not for another couple of months.'

'Yeah.' There was a pause.

'We're going out for dinner soon too.' Megan tried to change tack. 'The Ace of Hearts is having a salsa evening. Do you know it?'

Danny nodded. 'Too posh for me.'

'It's just for the salsa class,' said Megan. 'We're going as a group next month. It should be a really fun evening.'

'Yeah.' Danny sat back and gave a satisfied sigh. 'That was good. I could eat another whole one of those.' He looked up and smiled at Megan. 'You want me to call the agency and ask them if they'd take a look at you?' Megan looked blank. 'The modelling agency?' he prompted.

'Oh – uh, yeah, OK. That would be great.'

'Come on.' Danny got up. 'Let's go for a walk.'

It was a beautiful clear evening. 'Stars,' said Megan, looking up.

'Yeah. Not many, are there?'

'It's because of all the street lights. We could see loads more in Milton, where I used to live.' Megan felt sad as she said it.

Danny took her hand. 'You cold?'

'No, I'm fine.'

'Sorry about the show,' he said unexpectedly. 'I know you wanted to see it.'

'It's all right. I should have known you wouldn't like it.'

'I'm just not used to sitting still for so long.' He gave a sudden leap onto a low wall. 'My legs just want to keep moving. You know?' He did a kind of shuffle along the wall, then jumped straight up and landed securely in exactly the same place.

Megan laughed. 'You should do gymnastics.'

'Nah. Too much like ballet, all those tights and stuff.' Danny glanced ahead and his face lit up. 'You see that flight of steps?'

Megan nodded. About thirty metres ahead of them was a wide flight of stone steps leading up to Parchester's museum. 'What about them?'

'Someday I'm going to jump those on my board.'

Megan gaped. 'What, the whole flight? From the top to the bottom?'

'Yup. It can be done, I've seen people do it on YouTube.'

'But that must be . . . how many steps are there?'

'Twenty-six. I've counted them.' Danny grinned. 'I just have to get up enough speed. Paul's going to video me doing it.'

'But that's so dangerous.' Megan waved an arm at the road running past. 'Even if you jump the steps, you'll end up in the middle of the road. You could get run over!'

'I'll do it at night, duh,' said Danny, as though she were stupid. 'When there aren't so many cars around. Paul can be lookout. Or you can, if you want to come.'

'Me?'

'Yeah.' He grinned. 'Don't you want to see me jump this? It would be massive!'

Megan gazed at the flight of steps. She could just imagine Danny speeding towards it, kicking off from the ground . . . rising through the air . . . soaring above the steps . . . jolting to a triumphant landing . . . A tiny flame of excitement lit up inside her. It *would* be massive, he was right. Dangerous, of course – but imagine if he pulled it off! 'What if you crash? You could really hurt yourself. What if you break something?'

'Oh, I've done that before,' Danny said airily. 'My left arm twice, my right arm once, left ankle once too. And a couple of toes.' He smiled at her and jumped off the wall. 'Don't worry, I'm not asking if *you* want to jump the steps.'

'As if!'

He laughed. 'I think you need a bit more practice first, don't you?'

'Just a bit.'

He put his arms around her. 'Don't worry. I'll help you practise . . .' His eyes softened as he leaned towards her. '. . . All sorts of things . . .'

Megan closed her eyes. This was her chance to experience it all over again – kissing Danny. But instead of being lost in the moment, she found herself absurdly aware of her left foot, which was definitely lower than her right foot, even though she was standing with both feet firmly on the ground. Was she standing in a hole?

'Mmm,' said Danny, breaking away and gazing at her. 'You're a good kisser.'

Megan smiled. 'Thanks.' She leaned towards him again – maybe she could concentrate this time?

Danny's gaze flicked back to the stone steps. 'D'you think I should try to jump the railings at the sides too?'

'Huh?' Megan was taken aback. Didn't he want to kiss her again?

Danny was dragging her over to the steps. 'Look – they're not that high. It would make the jump even more awesome, wouldn't it?'

Megan made a non-committal reply. When she got a chance, she cast a quick look back at the pavement.

She was right; she had been standing in a hole.

Chapter 12

why can't you just stop interfering?

'Hey. Is now a good time?'

'Yeah, it's fine.' Jake sounded more cheerful this time. 'How's it going?'

'Great!' Megan hesitated for a moment, but then why shouldn't she tell him about Danny? He was her best friend, after all. 'I went out with Danny last night. You'll never guess what – he said I could be a model!'

Jake was amused. 'How would he know?'

'Oh, didn't I tell you? He does modelling himself. Him and his sister. Well, he says he gets more work than her because he's a boy. But he said I had really good bone structure and charisma.'

'Charisma?'

'Yeah, it's like when you can't take your eyes off someone. You know? When you look at them and go "wow".'

'Oh, right. I know what you mean.'

'Pardon?'

Jake cleared his throat. 'I said, I know what you mean.'

'So anyway, we went for an ice cream and a walk. And he was talking about this jump he wants to make on his skateboard – this massive flight of steps outside the museum. Totally mad – he could practically kill himself!'

'Whoa.'

'I know! He is so wild!'

'So you went out for ice cream?'

'N-no, we actually went to the theatre.'

'Oh?' She could tell Jake's ears had pricked up. 'What did you see?'

'*Riverdance*.' Megan squirmed slightly.

'Wow! You lucky thing! The only time it came anywhere near Milton, I was ill and couldn't go.' Jake sounded envious. 'What was it like?'

'Brilliant,' replied Megan. 'Really brilliant.'

'Did they do that thing at the end where they all line up and it's like they're almost robots because they're so perfectly in time?'

Megan bit her lip. 'Yeah. It was so amazing!' Why was she lying? She hadn't seen the end! But she knew if it had been Jake with her, they would both have been glued to their seats, eyes fixed to the stage for the whole performance.

Jake let out a breath. 'I am so jealous. They say it's the farewell tour. I don't suppose I'll get to see it now. Oh well. What did Danny think of it?'

Megan squeezed her eyes shut and crossed her fingers. 'He really enjoyed it,' she lied.

Jake waited for more but Megan didn't say anything else. 'And?' he prompted.

'And what?'

'Well – I don't know. Was it the first time he'd seen something like it? I mean he doesn't sound like the dancey type.'

'Oh,' said Megan miserably. 'Yeah, it was the first time. He was surprised by how much he liked it, actually.' She couldn't believe she was making all this up! But somehow if she told Jake the truth . . . She shook her head. She wanted to preserve the nice moments with Danny. And she wanted Jake to be impressed that she had a boyfriend. He wouldn't be impressed if he knew that Danny had made them leave at the interval, and Megan realized she really wanted Jake to like the sound of Danny. She wanted Jake to be happy for her.

'Well, that's great,' said Jake. 'It sounds like you're a perfect match.' He cleared his throat again.

'I think we are,' agreed Megan, though it sounded unconvincing to her own ears. Was that how she really felt?

There was silence for a moment.

'So when are you coming down?' asked Megan, attempting to change the subject. 'Mum's cleared most of the boxes out of the spare room and she says there will even be a bed in it by the time you arrive.' She laughed.

'Uh, well . . .' Jake took a breath. 'Thing is, Megan, I'm not sure I'm coming after all . . .'

Megan felt as though her stomach had suddenly become very heavy. 'What? Why not? I thought – I thought it was all settled.'

'Yeah. It's just that – um . . .' Jake seemed to be struggling for an answer. 'Well . . .'

A sudden thought struck Megan. 'Oh God! It's not – it's not because of your stepdad's redundancy, is it? I mean – is it a money thing?'

'Yes,' said Jake quickly, in some relief. 'Yes, that's it. We haven't got the money. I'm really sorry.'

'No, I'm sorry,' said Megan sincerely. 'I hadn't even thought . . . could we send you the money?'

'No,' said Jake. 'No, thanks anyway. Mum wouldn't take it.'

'I guess not. Oh, Jake.' Megan felt almost tearful.

'It's such bad news. I was so looking forward to you coming.'

'I know.' Jake's voice had steadied and he sounded genuinely sorry. 'I'm gutted too. Maybe we can meet up at Christmas or something?'

'Yeah, maybe.' Megan clutched the phone to her ear more tightly. 'You won't – forget me, will you?'

Jake burst out laughing, and then he sobered. 'Never, Meg. I could *never* forget you.'

♥

'I know it's a pain to move everything,' said Bryan, panting as he carried a chest of drawers out of Megan's room, 'especially as you've just got it all where you want it. But it'll make the painting so much faster and easier. We might even get it all done today.'

'Humph,' said Nicola disbelievingly. 'That sounds unlikely.'

'Can I help?' asked Owen, peering round the corner of the door, Snowy dangling from his hand by one leg. 'I'm good at painting.'

Nicola laughed. 'You certainly are, Owen. So I tell you what: you and me will have our own painting party downstairs.'

Owen pouted. 'I want to help Megan.'

Nicola looked helplessly at Megan.

'I'd love you to help,' said Megan to Owen. She crouched down. 'I'm only using one colour, though. Just lilac. Everything will be lilac.'

'Just lilac?' Owen looked perplexed. 'No red?'

'No.'

'Yellow?'

'No.'

'Blue?'

'No.'

Owen's face creased further as he tried to think of more colours. 'Orange?'

'No,' said Megan. 'But downstairs, Mummy's got all those colours. And more.'

'Really?'

'Yes. But I'd love you to help up here if you'd like to.' Megan held out a paintbrush.

Owen considered it for a moment before shaking his head. 'No thank you. I think I'll help Mummy downstairs.'

Megan pretended to look disappointed. 'Oh, all right. If you're sure.'

'I am.' Owen turned and headed down the stairs. 'Come on, Mummy.'

'See you later,' Nicola told the other two. 'Give me a yell if you need something.'

'Coffee?' suggested Bryan.

'Get it yourself,' retorted Nicola good-humouredly.

'Charming.'

Once Nicola had gone, Megan's dad opened the window and shook out the dustsheets. 'Got to cover everything up,' he told her. 'Paint is a bug— uh, very difficult to get out of a carpet.'

'You don't have to pretend not to swear in front of me,' said Megan. 'I have heard that word before, you know.'

'It's inbuilt,' said Bryan apologetically. 'When you have children, you soon learn that they repeat everything you say. I learned that the hard way.' He peered at her. 'Are you OK? You look a bit pale.'

'I'm all right.'

He looked sympathetic. 'You must be disappointed about Jake not coming down after all this week.'

'Yeah, I am. It's almost like we were never in Milton, Dad. Like we've got no connection any more.'

'You and Jake?' Bryan raised his eyebrows. 'I'd have said you had an unbreakable connection, what with your dancing and everything.'

'Not just Jake – everything back home. It's all different here. And as for dancing . . .' Megan sighed. 'I miss that too.'

Her father carefully tucked the dustsheet round

the edge of the carpet. 'I can see how it must be frustrating.' He frowned. 'We haven't done enough to find you a class. I've been so caught up in everything at work . . .'

'That's another thing,' said Megan. 'I think maybe Jake is jealous, just a tiny bit.'

'Of what? Of you?'

'Well, no – of you. You and your new job. Just as his stepdad has lost his.'

Bryan sat back on his heels. 'That's a real blow,' he admitted. 'Stephen's good, too. Very good. His company has missed a trick by losing him. I'd work with him anytime.'

'Maybe you could find him a job in your company?' suggested Megan, half-joking.

Her dad smiled. 'Think I'm still a bit too new to be making changes like that. I'm still finding my feet myself. Besides, it's a tight unit. No room for extra employees.'

Megan shrugged. Even though she hadn't really been serious, she felt a bit disappointed. 'Never mind. If Stephen's as good as you say, I'm sure he'll find another job soon.'

'Hmm.' Bryan seemed about to say something but changed his mind. 'Come on, let's get this paint pot open and get started.'

When Nicola came to see how they were getting on, the two of them were painting in concentrated silence, Bryan with his tongue sticking out as he negotiated a tricky window sill and Megan with lilac paint smudged across her cheek. 'This is looking better already!' Nicola stood in the middle of the room and gazed around. 'I wasn't sure about the colour at first, but you were right, Megan. It's lovely.'

Megan straightened up from her position on the floor. 'I like it too. Can I have new bedclothes to match?'

Her dad rolled his eyes. 'More money!' he complained, joking. 'Do you think I'm made of it?'

'Of course you can,' said her mum. 'But one thing at a time, OK? I came to ask if you'd like some sandwiches or something. Owen's watching *Monsters Inc.* so I've got a bit of time to make lunch.'

'That would be fab,' said Megan, putting her roller down in the paint tray.

'Don't stop yet.' Nicola held up a hand. 'You've got at least five minutes more while I go and make them. I'll bring them up so you only have to stop for a bit. I don't want to interrupt your flow!'

It wasn't until her mum brought the sandwiches up that Megan realized quite how hungry she was. 'Delicious!' proclaimed Bryan, munching away.

Nicola settled herself on the floor with them. 'Is Mari coming round to practise again this week, Megan? Only it would be good to know which evening so I don't plan something else for us instead.'

Megan shook her head. 'Not this week. She's gone away to visit grandparents for a few days, seeing as it's half-term.'

'What about Danny?' asked her dad casually. 'Do you want to ask him to come round?'

'Um . . .'

'That's a good idea,' said Nicola brightly. 'Why don't you ask him to lunch one day?'

'Well . . .' Megan fidgeted. She wasn't at all sure she was ready to bring Danny home to meet her parents. 'I think he's busy.' She saw her parents exchange a look. 'What?'

'Nothing, nothing,' said her father hastily. 'It's just it would be nice to get to know him a bit better, that's all. More than just saying "hello" and "goodbye" when we drop you off or pick you up.'

Nicola smiled. 'Yes – it's only that we don't really know him at all. And you're spending a lot of time with him now . . .'

Megan felt a spike of annoyance. 'So?'

Her mother shrugged. 'So it's nice to know who your daughter's hanging out with.'

Megan stared. 'Are you saying you have to check out my friends before I can hang out with them?'

Bryan tried to make his voice sound light. 'Not at all. Your mum didn't mean it like that.'

'Then what did she mean?' Megan asked testily.

'There's no need to get defensive,' said Nicola, her eyes narrowing. 'It's not an unusual thing to ask, you know. You hang out with Mari and we've met her and we like her. And this Danny – well, he's sort of becoming a boyfriend, isn't he?'

'What do you mean, *sort of*?'

'So,' her mother ploughed on, 'if he's important to you, then he's important to us too.'

Something in Megan rebelled. 'I don't see why,' she said. '*I'm* the one going out with him, not you.'

'Don't be ridiculous,' said her mother sharply. 'And don't take that tone with me. I just want to make sure you're choosing the right friends, that's all.'

'The right friends? What do you mean by the *right* friends?'

'Umm . . .' said Bryan. 'Maybe we should . . .'

'The right friends,' said Nicola, trying to sound calm, 'are people who care about you. And know how to treat people decently. And don't influence their friends into doing things they don't want to do. Or give them a bad attitude.'

'A *bad attitude?*' Megan's eyes were wide with angry astonishment. 'You don't know anything about Danny!'

'I know he likes skateboarding and racing and dangerous activities,' snapped her mother. 'And I want to make sure you're not being led down the wrong path.'

Megan stood up. 'I can't believe I'm hearing this! First you move me *two hundred miles* away from all my friends and everyone I know – and now you're telling me I can't choose my own friends *here?*'

'That's not what—'

'Why can't you just stop interfering?' Megan felt anger boiling up inside her. The date with Danny hadn't gone as expected. Jake had backed out of coming to stay. And here were her parents telling her she couldn't be trusted to choose her own boy-friend! 'It's none of your business who I hang around with! How do you think I felt, having to move so far away from everyone I care about? And now I've found some new friends and a boy who seems to like me and want to go out with me, and you're telling me you need to check everyone out first? What, like some kind of *vetting* process? To make sure they're all right to be my friends?' She glanced down at her half-eaten sandwich. 'I don't want any more. I'm going downstairs for a break.'

There was silence behind her.

♥

Megan didn't sleep well. Her room had stayed half painted and even though the window had been open, there was still a faint smell of fumes. Her head ached and she felt hotly guilty about what she had said to her parents. It wasn't their fault her dad's job had been so far away from home. And they *had* tried to make it as easy for her as possible. But now that she had started thinking about home, Megan found it hard to stop. There were so many memories . . .

. . . peering over the fence at the age of five, to see Jake prancing around the sun-baked garden completely naked . . .

. . . falling over in the playground and grazing the side of her face, and her friend Amanda rushing over to help, absolutely terrified . . .

. . . going to early ballroom lessons with Jake and bossing him around when he got it wrong . . .

. . . Jake's endless patience and good humour, even when she was being annoying . . .

. . . going to the end-of-year dance in the last year

of primary and Jake trying to kiss Amanda behind the Wendy House . . .

. . . Megan not speaking to Jake for a whole four hours as protest on behalf of Amanda . . .

. . . first day at secondary school and being so relieved to see the faces of her friends . . .

. . . the day Amanda fell off the vaulting horse in PE and broke her leg . . .

. . . taking part in the dance competition last year and Jake saying he wouldn't ever dance with anyone else . . .

. . . having to pack up everything in her old room and seeing it completely bare . . .

. . . saying goodbye to Jake . . .

Megan sat up, wiping tears from her face angrily. It was no good feeling sorry for herself, was it? She glanced at the clock. It was two in the morning. The house was quiet.

She texted Jake.

How RU? I am really missing home, things here not so gd 2day. Wish u cud hav come 2 stay.

Her thumb hesitated over the 'send' button. Was it really fair to send it? Jake already felt bad enough about not coming to stay, didn't he? And he was worried about his stepdad's job. It made her worries look rather pathetic.

She bit her lip and deleted the message. Jake had enough to worry about. She would just have to pull herself together for the moment. And apologize to her parents in the morning.

Chapter 13

you don't care about me

'We're going to do it on Sunday,' Danny told her at the park. It was Friday evening and the light was already fading. Megan shivered and wondered what time Samantha and Paul would want to get home and into the warm. Jasmine was nowhere to be seen, and Megan wondered if she had heard about the date at the theatre and was staying away on purpose.

'Do what?'

He looked exasperated. 'The jump. The one by the museum? Don't you remember?'

'Oh!' Megan's expression cleared. 'Of course I remember.'

Samantha, sitting on one of the ramps, examined her nails. 'It's the stupidest idea I've ever heard.'

Megan glanced at her curiously. 'Don't you think he can do it?'

Samantha's gaze flicked up. 'Of course he can't. He's an idiot. It'll be the swimming pool all over again.'

Megan looked bewildered. 'Swimming pool?'

'Remember that time I told you about?' Danny glanced at her. 'I hurt my knee a bit.'

Samantha snorted. 'A bit? Nearly smashed your kneecap, you mean.' She turned back to Megan. 'They told him if that had happened, he probably wouldn't be able to walk again.'

Danny rolled his eyes. 'Sam's exaggerating. They can re-build knees these days, you know.'

'Whatever.'

'Anyway, that was over a year ago,' Danny told Megan. 'I'm way better at jumps now.'

'And I'll be there,' added Paul.

'Filming the disaster,' commented Samantha. 'Video evidence to give to the police when they arrest him for dangerous activities or something.'

Megan shook her head. Why did Samantha have to make such personal digs at her brother? After all, the same could be said for Paul, surely? He liked skating and all the same things Danny did. If Samantha disapproved so much of these activities, why was she going out with him? 'Why are you here?' The words were out before she'd even thought about them.

Samantha's steely gaze swung across again, fixing her in its beam. 'What do you mean?'

Megan sucked in her breath sharply. She hadn't

meant to say it out loud! 'Well,' she said, trying to be polite, 'it just seems a bit odd, that's all. You don't like skateboarding. And it's dark and getting cold out now. Why don't you just stay home?'

Megan hadn't thought Samantha could possibly look shocked by anything. Her oh-so-cool exterior seemed to bounce all emotion off it, like thick plastic. But Samantha looked shocked now. 'What's it got to do with *you*?' she asked, wrinkling her nose as if Megan smelled bad.

Megan glanced at Danny, suddenly uncomfortable. Maybe she had gone too far? But Danny didn't even seem to be listening. He was down on the ground again, screwdriver in hand and tinkering with the trucks on his skateboard.

Samantha stood up slowly, unfolding herself so that it was very obvious that she was at least four inches taller than Megan. 'Who do you think you are anyway?' she said in a venomous tone. 'Swanning around as though you're the new heroine around here. Trying to look cool on a skateboard. Who do you think you're impressing? My brother? Don't make me laugh. He only cares about things with wheels.'

Megan threw another glance in Danny's direction, but he was determinedly ignoring his sister. *Isn't he going to defend me?* she thought, suddenly annoyed.

He was only five or six steps away, he must be able to hear every word!

Samantha gave a derisive snort. 'Thought you were going to be the new sweetheart in the playground, didn't you?' She looked Megan up and down. 'You remind me of someone. Someone who crossed me not long ago. She regretted it too.'

'Would that be Fliss?' Megan asked, folding her arms. 'The girl you hurt in the summer?'

Samantha barely blinked. 'She thought she was so cool. It seems to be an epidemic around here. Small girls getting up my nose.' She sniffed.

'Maybe that's because your nose is too big,' said Megan, feeling more and more annoyed by the second. Why wasn't Danny stepping in to prevent his girlfriend from being insulted? 'And from what I heard, your plan backfired in a really big way. Nearly got arrested, that's what I heard.'

Samantha's cheeks burned a fiery pink. 'That's not true,' she said furiously.

'Lost your pocket money too,' added Megan, unable to resist the dig. 'No wonder you're hanging around with Paul. Hoping for a handout, are you?'

WHAP!

Megan's hand went automatically to her stinging cheek. Her jaw dropped. 'You *hit* me!'

Samantha too was looking a bit stunned. 'That's for what you said.'

'Which part?' retorted Megan, still holding her face. 'For calling you a charity case or for saying you nearly got arrested?'

Samantha opened her mouth but she didn't seem to know what to say. Instead, she simply glared at Megan. 'I don't have to listen to this,' she snapped, and turned to go. 'Come on, Paul.'

'Huh?' Paul looked up from his board as Samantha strode past. 'Where?'

'With me. Come *on*.' Paul quickly picked up his board and followed her obediently, throwing an apologetic glance over his shoulder at Danny.

There was silence for a moment as Megan watched Samantha and Paul disappear round the end of the children's playground. She rubbed her cheek ruefully. 'That really hurt.'

Danny put down his screwdriver and stood on his board, rocking it experimentally from side to side. 'Well, you did provoke her.'

Megan stared at him. '*What?*'

He shrugged and gave a laugh. 'Sam's got a nasty temper on her. Best not to get in her way.'

'Are you saying I *deserved* it?' Megan couldn't believe it.

'Course not. But Sam wouldn't see it like that.' He pushed off and started to head towards a ramp at the far end of the park.

'How come you didn't back me up?' Megan called after him.

'What?'

'Back me up. You know – how come you let her get away with saying all that?' Megan was beginning to feel annoyed all over again.

'Watch me take these two at once!' Danny called back as he raced towards the set of railings. He flew into the air but caught the edge of one of the railings with a back wheel and tumbled to the ground, laughing.

Megan stomped over, determined not to drop the subject. 'Danny. How come you let her insult me like that?'

He brushed the dirt off his jeans and looked up at her. 'What do you mean?'

'All that stuff she was saying. About me trying to be cool and how stupid I was.'

Danny raised his eyebrows. 'Sounded like you were fighting your own battle.' He grinned. 'That's what she didn't like. She's not used to people standing up to her. That jibe about her pocket money! No wonder you got slapped.' He laughed again.

In that small moment, it was as though someone had switched on a huge floodlight. Megan suddenly saw things with a clarity that had escaped her before. 'You don't care about me,' she said, surprised.

Danny frowned. 'Huh?'

'You don't.' Megan felt something like wonder. 'You don't care about anyone. Not me, not your sister, not Paul. Not Jasmine.'

'Why should I care about Jasmine?'

'Exactly.' Out of the blue, she felt like she wanted to laugh too. 'You don't notice anything going on around you. Everything is about *you* – about racing, about speed.'

Danny got to his feet. 'What's wrong with that?'

Megan shook her head. 'What about me?'

He frowned. 'What *about* you?'

A bubble of laughter popped out of Megan's throat. 'I thought I was supposed to be your girlfriend.'

'My what?' He stared at her. 'What made you think that?'

The laughter stopped. Megan's eyes opened wide. 'We went out together. We – you kissed me.'

He shrugged. 'So?'

'You mean . . . what did *you* think, then?'

'I just thought you were up for a good time,' Danny said carelessly. 'I thought you were cool about it all.' He screwed up his nose. 'I didn't realize you were going to get all uptight. What does it matter anyway?'

'*What does it matter?*' Megan stared. How could she possibly explain? *You made me feel alive*, she wanted to say. *You made me realize my life was tame and boring. You showed me new exciting things. You* kissed *me!* 'I thought you liked me,' she said lamely, and then felt cross with herself for sounding so pathetic. How could she have been so stupid for thinking she meant something to him?

Danny gave a massive sigh of exasperation. 'What is it with you girls?' He sounded annoyed. 'Why do you have to make such a big deal about everything? I *did* like you. You were up for a laugh. You liked trying out stuff. You were good to talk to. I didn't realize you were going to end up like all the rest of them.'

'All the rest of them?' Megan repeated, bewildered.

'All those other girls.' Danny swung out an arm. 'Hanging on my every word. Wanting to follow me around all the time. Hold my hand. Crying if I don't call them. You're all the same!'

'Hang on a minute.' Megan's stupefaction was slowly turning to anger. 'How many other girls have you been out with?'

Danny shrugged. 'I dunno. I dumped them all. They got boring.'

'*Boring*?' Megan almost choked. 'Why, because they wanted to be your girlfriend?'

'What is it with all the labels?' Danny retorted. 'Why does it matter to you girls about that kind of thing? If you like each other, then you can hang out together. Why does it have to get boyfriend–girlfriend complicated? Isn't it enough to like hanging out together?'

Megan suddenly remembered Mari saying almost exactly the same thing: 'What's the big deal anyway?' She opened her mouth to reply, but then it struck her: maybe *she* was the one who had got it wrong? Were Danny and Mari right; was it enough just to hang out together and be good friends?

But I have that already, she thought. *I have friends I hang out with and have a laugh with. I did that with Jake for years!*

And now I want the other thing. The relationship, boyfriend–girlfriend thing. I want it all – the holding hands, the sweet conversations. I want to walk in the moonlight, on the beach, through a forest. Like they do in books and films and songs. What's so wrong with that?

And then another thought came out of the blue:

Jake would never have treated me like this. The idea startled her.

Megan took a deep breath. 'I don't think we should hang out together any more,' she said, and was amazed at how calm her voice sounded.

Danny nodded. 'You said it. I thought you were different. I thought you were like me. But it turns out you're just the same as all the other wimpy girls. Just like Jasmine. She fell apart too.'

'Jasmine?' Megan was momentarily diverted. 'You – did you go out with Jasmine?'

'Once,' said Danny. 'A while back. But I moved on and she – she just kept hanging around, like a bad smell.'

'How can you talk about people that way?' Megan cried. 'How can you treat them like that? Jasmine never stops watching you. She's crazy about you, and you ignore her the whole time! I guess she's just hoping that one day you'll take her back. Well, I hope for her sake you never do. Because you'll just treat her like a doormat to wipe your feet on – all over again. And she's miserable enough already. You can't *do* that to people, Danny.'

'Listen to you!' Danny's eyes suddenly blazed. 'Lecturing me about how to behave! When all you ever do is moan! "Oh, my ponytail hurts under the helmet." "You shouldn't do that, it's dangerous." "Why don't you want to watch the rest of the stupid dance show?"' His face twisted in disgust.

'Dancing is not stupid! You know nothing about it!'

'And I don't want to!' he snapped back. 'Not if it's anything like that boring drivel you made me sit through at the theatre. God! Why would anyone want to *do* something like that? What a waste of time!'

'I love it!' Megan could hear her heart thumping in her ears. 'I'd been really looking forward to it! And you ruined it all! By not being able to sit still! What are you – a *child*?'

Danny took a step forward so that his face was up close to hers. Megan flinched at the ferocity in his expression. 'You know *nothing* about me. You know nothing about where I've come from; what me and Sam have been through. Oh, poor Megan, who had to move fifty million miles away from her ickle friends. Poor, lonely Megan with her boring life. Try being taken away from your parents when you were little and put in care for two years! Try having to look after your sister when she was picked on and bullied by all the other kids! Try having to make nice with your parents again when you finally get out, when all the time you just want to smash their faces in for messing your life up!'

Megan was completely astonished, and not a little afraid. She swallowed. 'What are you talking about?'

'Oh no.' Danny shook his head, though the flame in his eyes still burned. 'You don't get to feel sorry for me. Don't you *dare* try to be sympathetic. I might have let you once – back when I thought you were still cool, still different from the rest. But not now. You run off home – go back to your ballet shoes and your stupid dancing. I don't know why I wasted my time on you. And as for kissing you – yeuch!' He made a face. 'It was disgusting.'

Megan felt as though all the air had rushed out of her lungs. *Disgusting?* Kissing her was *disgusting?* Was that true? Her knees felt weak and her head was spinning. She couldn't possibly answer him. Cheeks burning and eyes wet, she dropped her head and turned.

'That's right,' came Danny's voice from behind her, softer now but no less menacing. 'Get back to your cosy little life. You don't belong here.'

Megan ran out of the skate park, stumbling twice as her vision blurred. She blinked rapidly. She must not cry in front of Danny! She felt humiliated enough; she refused to give him that pleasure.

She rounded the corner of the park and ran straight into someone coming the other way. Confused memories rushed through her head – it was only a couple of months since she had first met Danny this way – but this person was a girl, and she was struggling out of the hedge, cursing.

'Jasmine!'

Jasmine glanced up at Megan, annoyed, but the words froze on her lips. 'Megan.' She hesitated. 'You OK?'

Megan rubbed her eyes hastily. 'I'm fine. Got to get home.'

'Wait.' Jasmine grabbed her arm. 'Is this – I don't mean to – is it Danny?'

'He's the most selfish person I've ever met,' snapped Megan.

'I know.' Jasmine nodded. She dropped Megan's arm. 'Sorry.'

'You *know*?' Megan stared. 'Then why on earth are you still hanging around him? When he treats you like – like *that*?'

Jasmine shrugged pathetically. 'I can't help it. He's – he's like a bright light. I can't stay away.' She gazed anxiously at Megan. 'You won't tell?'

'Who would I tell?' Megan replied. 'I'm not coming back here.' Then, seeing Jasmine's expression, she softened. 'Of course I won't tell. But you should get away from him too, you know. He's no good. Not a good person.' She shivered. 'And there's a lot of stuff under there. I didn't know. But it's not good. He's so *angry*.'

Jasmine screwed up her face. 'Not sure I'm a good person either.' She gave a half-hearted laugh. 'Maybe it's what I deserve.'

'No, you don't,' Megan started to say, but Jasmine had already turned away and was heading into the skate park. Towards the solitary figure of Danny, practising his jumps as usual.

Megan felt something like a sharp pain in the side of her ribs. Standing here, at the edge of the skate park, nearly out of sight, it was almost as though she were at some kind of crossroads in her life. *What do I want?* she wondered. *Do I want excitement? Do I want exhilaration that's closer to terror? Do I want a boyfriend more than anything?*

She glanced up at the sky. It was darkening fast now, and the street light above her head flickered on. 'I want to go home,' Megan said out loud, to the light. And then, 'I want to talk to Jake.'

Chapter 14

you can't let him do this to you!

'What's the matter?' Jake's voice was alarmed. 'You sound really upset.'

Megan sniffed. 'I sort of broke up with Danny. Well, he broke up with me, actually.'

'Oh.' Jake paused for a moment. 'Oh, Megan, I'm really sorry. What happened?'

'Wouldn't *you* think,' Megan said crossly, 'that if you go on dates with someone and you kiss them, that they're your girlfriend?'

'Umm . . .' said Jake cautiously. 'Yeah, I guess so.'

'I mean, was I really dim to think we were *going out* going out?' Megan went on, reaching for a tissue at the same time. 'We went out together, just us, *alone*. To do things and see stuff. I mean, that's a date, isn't it?'

'Er . . .'

'And he said he liked me. Lots of times. He said I had charisma. He said I should do modelling. Wouldn't *you* think,' Megan blew her nose, 'that meant he fancied me?'

'I would, yes. Er – did he say he didn't fancy you after all then?'

'He didn't say *exactly* that.' Megan threw the tissue at the bin and missed. 'Blast. He started going on about how easy my life was and how pathetic it was to like dancing and why had I wanted to take him to that stupid dance show in the first place— Oh!'

'What?' Jake was startled. 'I thought you said he liked *Riverdance*?'

Megan pulled another tissue from its box. 'I wasn't totally telling the truth,' she admitted. 'He didn't like it. He made me leave at the interval.'

'He did *what*?'

'I know.'

'Oh, Meg, so you had to miss the second half?'

'Yes.' Megan blew her nose again. 'And I thought it was just because he hated being cooped up and sitting in those seats, but *actually* he was acting like a spoiled child and I hate him now.'

'That's really bad luck.'

'I do, I hate him. And his stupid sister. I should have known. Mari told me what they were like.'

'What do you mean?'

'Mari – you know, the girl from salsa – she told me this awful story about Samantha that happened in the summer. Their drama group was doing a play and she put oil on a ladder so this girl would fall off and get hurt and Samantha could play her part.'

'Which girl?' asked Jake, bewildered. 'What part?'

'Mari's friend Fliss,' said Megan in frustration, 'aren't you listening? She was playing Juliet and she fell off the ladder and she nearly died, and Mari told me not to trust Samantha and she said if Danny was her brother then he'd be just as bad . . .'

'Whoa, whoa!' cried Jake. 'Time out! I'm not following this at all.'

'Sorry.' Megan took a breath. 'It doesn't matter anyway. And I think there was a whole load of stuff that was kind of simmering under the surface all the time. Danny said something about him and Samantha being in care when they were little.'

'Oh,' said Jake. 'That doesn't sound good.'

'I know. I would have felt sorry for him . . . but he got really angry with me.' Megan's voice wobbled. 'I was a bit scared, actually.'

'Meg, it's not your fault.' Jake was warm and reassuring. 'It sounds like you're better off without him, if you don't mind my saying.'

Megan nodded, even though she knew Jake couldn't

see her. 'I know. I'm sure you're right. I just feel so stupid. And so embarrassed.'

'Well, you shouldn't be,' said Jake firmly. 'If he couldn't appreciate you for who you are then he's not worth bothering about.'

Megan smiled. 'Thanks. That's a really sweet thing to say.'

'Well,' Jake said gruffly, 'you'd make a great girl-friend. I think.' There was a voice in the background suddenly and Jake said, 'Hang on, Meg.' There was a muffled discussion and then he came back on the line. 'Sorry, Megan, I've got to go. Skye's here.'

'Who?'

'Skye. The girl from next door, remember? We're going bowling.'

'Oh.' Megan was startled. 'What, just the two of you?'

'No, no. There's a whole bunch. But since we live next door to each other, we're going together. You know, like you and me used to. Listen, I've got to run. But give me a call tomorrow, OK? And cheer up. He's not worth it.'

Megan opened her mouth to say 'goodbye' but Jake had already gone. She stared at her phone in aston-ishment and not a little confusion. Jake was going to things with Skye, the girl from next door – 'like you and me used to'. Megan wasn't at all sure how she felt about that. Had Jake found a replacement for her already? It felt like a betrayal! She was surprised how jealous she was.

The front door bell rang, but Megan hardly noticed. It was only when her mother called up, 'Mari's here!' that Megan looked round.

There were thumping footsteps on the stairs, and then Mari's head appeared in the doorway. 'Hey, how's it going? I know it's kind of late but Mum said I could drop in while she was at Tesco because there's something vitally important we have to discuss. And your mobile was engaged.' Her eyes widened. 'Hey, are you OK? You look like you've been crying.'

Megan wiped her eyes. 'Oh, it's nothing really.'

'What did she do?' Mari demanded, joining Megan on the bed.

'Who?'

'Samantha, of course. What did she say to you?'

Megan's jaw dropped. 'Well, it wasn't *her* exactly. I mean, it was a bit . . .'

'Tell me *everything*,' Mari ordered.

And to her surprise Megan found herself spilling out the whole story. Mari was a good listener, but she was inclined to exclaim 'No way!' rather too often.

'I warned you,' she said when Megan had finished

the sorry tale. 'I told you what Samantha was like. I still can't believe she hit you though. That is *so* out of order.' She peered at Megan's face. 'I can't see a mark though. That's lucky.'

'I'm not really that bothered by Samantha,' Megan said in a wobbly voice. 'It's more what Danny said.'

'But you can't believe anything he said.' Mari flapped a hand as though swatting him away. 'The world revolves around Danny, according to him anyway. He's a Brooks.'

'He said I was pretty,' said Megan lamely.

'You *are* pretty!'

'You just said I couldn't believe anything he said.'

'*Well.*' Mari took a breath. 'All right, you can believe *some* things. The bits that are true, anyway. But not the bits you know are rubbish. Come on, do you seriously believe *Riverdance* is boring drivel?'

'Of course not.'

'There you go.'

'But Mari . . .' Megan's lip wobbled, and her voice dropped. 'He said kissing me was disgusting.'

'Oh, Megan.' Mari sounded kind. 'Do you honestly think that's likely? He just said that to hurt you.'

'What if it's true? What if – what if no one will want to kiss me ever again?'

'You need a night out with the girls,' said Mari

firmly. 'And luckily, that's exactly what we're doing tomorrow! It's our night out with the salsa group!'

'Oh.' Megan had completely forgotten. 'I don't think I want to go.'

'Why not?'

'I don't feel up to it. You go. I'm sure it'll be a great night.'

'Now you listen to me.' Mari put on a strict expression. 'It's salsa night. It's *dancing*. Dancing will cheer you up, right? It's the best cure for feeling down, you know it is.'

'I don't think . . .'

'You're being ridiculous!' Mari exploded. 'You can't let him do this to you! Listen, Megan . . . if you don't come out with us, then *he's won*. You hear me? Danny wanted to make you feel bad. He *wants* you to stay home moping because he's dumped you. If you do that – well then, he's the winner, isn't he? Are you really going to let him beat you?'

'Um . . .'

'If Sean dumped *me*,' Mari said, her voice rising, 'I would be out partying *that very night*! Just to show him! Not that he would dump me. No chance of *that*.'

Megan was puzzled. 'You sound like you *want* him to dump you.'

'No, I don't really.' Mari gave a frustrated sigh. 'Though in some ways it might make things easier. He's always hanging around, that's all. He doesn't give me any space.'

'He *likes* you, Mari.'

'But he doesn't have to smother me, does he?' Mari demanded. Then she laughed. 'Look at us – we've got opposite problems!'

'I guess so.' Megan gave a half-smile, despite herself. She was beginning to feel as though breaking up with Danny might not be the end of the world after all.

'So you'll come?' Mari returned to her original topic. 'Tomorrow?' She grabbed Megan's hands. 'Please say you will. I promise we'll have a fab time.'

'Well . . .'

'Remember what I said. If you don't come, he's won. Don't let him destroy you.'

Megan couldn't help but laugh. 'You are so over-dramatic. All right. I'll come.'

Mari let out a whoop. 'Excellent! Can't wait!'

Chapter 15

we're strictly friends

'This is amazing,' Mari remarked, beaming from ear to ear.

'What?'

'I SAID,' Mari bellowed, 'this is AMAZING!'

'Oh! Yeah!' Megan nodded enthusiastically.

The Ace of Hearts restaurant had been transformed into a Caribbean paradise. Plastic palm trees were attached to every pillar, while waiters moved smoothly around carrying coconut shells with various cocktails. Cuban music was blasting out of the speakers, and a large dance area had been cleared in the middle of the room.

Megan felt her spirits rise. Mari had been right, this was just what she needed to cheer herself up. Her feet were already tapping of their own accord as the music pounded through her body.

'This way!' Corinne waved the group of girls over to a large table in the corner of the room. 'I brought my friend Candy along to keep us company.'

Candy, who had pink stripes through her hair and an open, friendly face, waved at them from her place at the table and seemed particularly pleased to see Mari. 'I didn't realize you had taken up dance, Mari.'

'You wouldn't have thought it, would you?' agreed Mari. 'Not after the mess I made of dance rehearsals in *Romeo and Juliet*.' She turned to Megan. 'Candy directed the play in the summer.'

'I didn't realize,' Corinne was saying loudly, 'but there are guest dancers too. Before we eat.'

'Brilliant!' Mari clapped her hands. 'This is the most exciting evening I've had since . . . the last exciting evening!'

Megan laughed. It felt so good to be out with friends again! She leaned forward eagerly as the music suddenly stopped and a man stepped into the middle of the dance floor to introduce the guest dancers. 'Please welcome the Junior Latin Champions, Sylvia Palazzo and Cesar Mulligan!'

Megan's jaw dropped. 'I know them!' she whispered excitedly to Mari as two teenagers took up position on the floor.

'No way!'

'They were at a competition up north last year! I

was entering with Jake, and they were in the exhibition. They're amazing!'

The music started, and the two dancers began to move. Megan sat spellbound; they were even better than she remembered! Beside her, she heard Mari breathe out, 'Wow!'

The routine was so fast and so exciting, Megan felt an almost uncontrollable urge to get up and join in. Sylvia and Cesar's arms and legs were a blur as they tangled together and then always inexplicably came free again. Sylvia's tiny Latin dress was covered with sequins and feathers and glittered in the mirror ball above the dance floor. Cesar's black suit had flames of red licking up the sides and he whipped around the floor as though he were dancing on air.

When the music finished and the dancers struck their final pose, the place erupted in cheers and applause. Megan and Mari got to their feet automatically, cheering as loudly as anyone else. Sylvia and Cesar bowed to all four sides of the floor and then went off, waving and smiling.

'That was AMAZING,' declared Mari. The rest of the girls around the table looked as excited as she was.

'Did you see her *feet*?' asked Alys.

'Did you see her *dress*?'

'Did you see her *hips*?'

'I was too busy looking at him,' Jackie said, shrugging. The others laughed.

'He was totally hot,' Mari agreed. 'And Megan actually *knows* him!'

The other girls gasped and turned to Megan, agog. 'No way!'

'I don't actually *know* him,' Megan admitted. 'I mean, he's not a friend or anything. But I've met them both before. At a competition last year. They were really nice.'

The other girls looked impressed, and Megan blushed. She hoped no one thought she was showing off.

'So, girls, you think you can do something like that at Christmas?' Corinne broke in, grinning.

'*What*?' Mari looked aghast. 'You are joking.'

Corinne laughed. 'All right, maybe I won't expect quite that standard this Christmas. Maybe by next year . . . ?'

'Yeah, right,' Mari scoffed. 'I couldn't be that good if I practised for *twenty* years.'

'I wouldn't mind trying that twisty thing they did with their arms,' Alys said. 'You know, where she sort of went under his arms, like loops . . .'

The discussion turned technical.

'One thing's for sure,' said Mari decidedly. 'We have to have one of *those*.' She pointed at the mirror ball hanging over the dance floor.

Corinne laughed. 'They're expensive, Mari. And complicated to light.'

'I don't care.' Mari looked obstinate. 'We can't have a Christmas dance party without a mirror ball.'

Megan grinned. 'Agreed.'

Corinne rolled her eyes, amused. 'All right. I'll see what I can do.'

Dinner was a mixture of Mexican and Caribbean food, in keeping with the salsa theme. 'Delicious,' mumbled Mari, her mouth full of chicken fajita. 'Pass that fried banana stuff.'

The conversation was serious and silly by turns, and Megan couldn't remember the last time she had laughed so much. By the time dessert was being cleared away, she wasn't at all sure she'd be able to move, let alone dance.

'Oof.' Mari echoed her thoughts. 'I must have put on at least a stone.' She patted her stomach. 'But it was worth it.'

'You can work it all off again when we start dancing,' Megan told her.

Mari looked horrified. 'I can't possibly dance, I'll be sick.'

'I danced once when I was sick,' Megan said, remembering. 'Properly ill, I mean. With flu. It was horrible. And I didn't do very well anyway. I should have just stayed home.'

Mari sat forward. 'So tell us about this competition where you met those two dancers. Last year.'

'Oh, it was just a competition I entered with Jake,' Megan said. 'It wasn't very special really.'

'Jake?' Jackie had pricked up her ears. 'Is this your mythical dance partner from the wilds of Yorkshire?'

Megan laughed. 'Not exactly wild. In fact, you can't get much further from "wild" if you're talking about Jake.'

'What's he like?' Mari asked.

Megan pushed her hair behind her ear. 'He's – he's just *Jake*,' she said, shrugging. 'He's my best friend.'

Mari pulled a face. 'That's no good, Meg. Come on, you'll have to do better than that. What's he look like, for a start?'

Megan considered for a moment. 'Well, he's got brown eyes and brown hair. Sort of sticky-up on top, you know, the sort of hair that never lies flat, even if you cover it in hair gel. We had real trouble getting it to look posh for competitions.' She giggled. 'At one competition, they had called our names about three times and we were still trying to stick Jake's hair down

214

because we were doing the tango and it had to be all slicked back. In the end, my mum got so exasperated she emptied a pot of my little brother's glue over Jake's head.'

'She tipped glue on him?' Mari snorted. 'Did it work?'

'It did actually,' said Megan, 'though we got seriously told off by the floor manager because we were late for our slot and they had to wait for us. We placed third though, so it was worth it. Though' – she grinned – 'it took him half an hour of solid shampooing to get all the glue out. And in the end he had to use Fairy Liquid! He complained he smelled like an air freshener for the next week!' Megan felt a warmth spread through her, the way it always did when she thought about Jake. 'He's really nice, Mari. You'd love him.'

'What about you?' Mari asked curiously.

'What do you mean?'

'Haven't you ever – been out with him?'

Megan shook her head. 'It's not like that. We're strictly friends. He's sweet and kind and makes me laugh, but we've never gone out.'

'Sounds to me like he'd be the perfect boyfriend,' commented Mari.

Alys, who had been listening in, nodded. 'And he

can dance too! He's like the perfect match for you, Megan.'

Megan tried to laugh. 'Oh, I don't think of him that way. We've never been . . . you know.' But inside, something was flickering like a tiny flame. Why *hadn't* they ever gone out? Alys's words struck a chord. They did make the perfect couple, didn't they?

Mari raised her eyebrows. 'Well, if you ask me, he'd be much better for you than . . . *you know who.*'

Megan shrugged and tried to sound casual. 'He's my best friend. I wouldn't want to spoil that. Besides, he lives two hundred miles away now.' Her mind was spinning. It was almost as though the pieces of her life were shifting and coming down in a different pattern . . . what *would* it be like to go out with Jake?

Mari said nothing, but Megan saw her exchange glances with Alys. There was no time for further conversation anyway because just then the sound system blared into life again, and the infectious Cuban rhythms soon had everyone leaping for the dance floor, full stomachs or not!

The girls from the salsa class more than held their own on the dance floor. Jackie managed to find herself a cute boy to dance with, even though their dancing seemed to consist more of jumping up and down than actual salsa. Mari, having declared herself far too shy to dance in public, was the most outrageous of them all! She shimmied and swung, waved her arms around like a maniac and shouted with joy at the top of her voice. Megan laughed at the sight of her friend having so much fun. 'Can't all our classes be like this?' Mari yelled to Corinne.

Corinne, face flushed and swaying with the rest of them, smiled. 'I wish!' she called back. 'Think how much your lessons would cost then!'

Time flew by in a haze of music and heat. Megan couldn't believe it when she looked at her watch and realized it was ten p.m. 'Time to go!' Corinne was calling to the girls, whose faces dropped with disappointment when they heard her.

Mari pulled her mobile phone out of her bag and then grimaced. 'My battery's dead. Megan, can I borrow yours?'

Megan dug around in her bag. 'Yeah, of course. Here you go. Isn't your mum picking you up as arranged then?'

Mari avoided her gaze. 'No, I said I'd call her when we were leaving. It's only five minutes in the car.' She glanced at the phone. 'No signal in here. I'll just be a minute.'

'Oh, right.' Megan thought it was a bit odd, but

Mari disappeared out of the front doors, Megan's mobile clutched in her hand. Megan busied herself making sure she had everything in her bag and that she'd handed the money over to Corinne for dinner as agreed.

Mari reappeared within minutes. She handed the phone back to Megan. 'Thanks.'

'No problem.' Megan vaguely noticed that the screen was showing 'Address Book'. Mari must have knocked the button when she finished her call. Megan quickly cancelled it and re-locked the keypad.

The group made their way out to the street, chatting and laughing. Stepping outside was like stepping into a fridge, though, and within minutes people were hurriedly waving goodbye and getting into warm cars with waiting parents. 'See you at salsa.' Mari gave Megan a hug.

'Your mum's here already?' asked Megan. 'Wow, that was quick.'

'Uh – yeah. Um . . . it went to voicemail when I rang; she must have already set off. Well, see you! Hope you've got that jive routine all ready for us!' Mari waved and ran off.

Megan saw Bryan sitting in his car on the other side of the road. 'Thanks, Corinne,' she said. 'That's my dad over there.'

Corinne gave her an unexpected hug. 'Really glad you came, Megan. I hope you had a good time.'

'I did, thanks.' Megan smiled. 'It was fab.' She crossed to the car.

'Had a good time?' Bryan asked. 'Actually, don't answer that. I can see you glowing from the inside out.'

Megan got into the welcoming warmth of the car. 'You know what, Dad? That's the best time I've had since we moved to Parchester.'

'I'm glad. Looks like you've found a nice bunch of friends there too.'

'Yeah, I have. I'm sorry about what I said the other day.'

'You've already apologized, Megan, you don't have to do it again.'

'I know. I just wanted to say it's not all bad here.'

Her dad reached over to pat her hand. 'I know it's been hard for you, being uprooted from everyone you knew. I'm really proud of the way you've coped. And if it's any consolation, I don't have any concerns at all about *this* group of friends.'

Megan grinned back at him. 'Me neither.' But on the way home, she found herself thinking not of her new friends but of Jake.

That tiny nagging flame inside – was it trying to

tell her something? All this time she'd thought of Jake as a friend . . . had she been completely wrong? Was he really the perfect match for her?

She'd known him for most of her life. He was her closest friend, the one she turned to when she needed advice or a shoulder to cry on. He knew her better than anyone. They had shared so much over the years . . . birthdays, Christmases, holidays, school . . . and dancing.

Dancing with Jake had always been the best feeling. They seemed to move instinctively together, almost as though their feet had some kind of telepathy. Dancing without him felt wrong, as though a part of her was missing. And Megan realized she didn't want to dance with anyone else – how could any other partner ever know her as well as Jake did? She couldn't believe that they wouldn't ever dance together again . . . surely that was impossible! They were partners for life, weren't they?

Partners for life . . . was it, perhaps, *more* than dancing that they shared? Did she, deep down, have feelings for him? Feelings that she had never really admitted were there?

Danny had been wrong for her; she could see that now. He was exciting and fresh and new, but he didn't care about people around him. He hadn't cared about

Megan's feelings; her hopes and dreams. Whereas Jake had always shared them, rejoiced in them – mainly because they had always been the same dreams as his. She couldn't imagine life without him.

Oh goodness! Megan bit her lip as she stared out of the car window. *Do I like Jake as more than just a friend? Have I been completely and utterly blind? Was there a moment in the past when I should have said or done something different?*

'Why are you shaking your head?' Her dad's voice broke into her thoughts.

'Was I? Oh – oh, no reason.'

But there *was* a reason. Megan had been thinking that even if she did feel more for Jake than friendship, there was absolutely nothing she could do about it.

Because one thing was for certain: Jake was two hundred miles away and it was far too late to change things now.

Chapter 16

do you fancy me?

'. . . And so I said that if they didn't put me in for the exam, I wouldn't dance in the Christmas Show,' finished Suki.

'Huh?'

Suki frowned. 'Megan, weren't you listening? I was saying I wouldn't do the show.'

'Which show?'

'The one at Christmas.' Suki looked cross. 'You didn't hear a word I said, did you?'

'Sorry.' Megan rubbed her eyes. 'I was choreographing the jive last night and then I couldn't get to sleep for ages.'

'You don't listen very well, do you?' commented Suki waspishly. 'Friends are supposed to listen to each other.'

Megan thought this was a bit rich, coming from Suki, who never seemed to listen to anything Megan said! 'I'm tired.'

Suki stood up, hefting her bag over her shoulder. 'You need some make-up. You've got dark circles under your eyes. I'll see you in registration.'

Megan sat at the lunch table for a few more minutes, staring into space. It was true, she was exhausted. And she knew she had dark circles under her eyes. She had spent several sleepless nights wondering about Jake and whether she'd blown her only chance. The more she thought about him, the more obvious it seemed that they were meant to be together. But it was also more and more obvious that there was nothing she could do. It was too late. So why was she wasting so much time and energy wondering about what might have been?

The bell went and Megan got up with a sigh. She needed to concentrate on the jive she was working on and not get distracted by thoughts of Jake. She had only a few weeks in which to teach the routine to the other girls.

'Hey! Is this your bag?'

Megan turned to see a short girl with a head of out-of-control brown curls holding up her school bag. 'Oh! Thanks so much, Kate. I don't know how I could have forgotten that!'

'You were thinking about something else,' offered

Kate with a smile. 'I do that all the time. Especially at school. Let's face it, there's not much to get excited about here, is there?'

Megan smiled back. 'Not really. I was thinking about dancing.'

The girl raised her eyebrows. 'Oh, right. You into ballet like Suki?'

'No,' said Megan shortly. Then she realized she might have sounded rude. 'I do ballroom dancing.'

'Of course. I remember you asking me about classes a while back. Did you get it sorted?'

'Not exactly.'

'I can't dance for anything,' Kate said ruefully. 'Look at my feet, they're huge.'

Megan glanced down. 'They don't look that big.'

'Size eight,' said Kate. 'Clodhoppers. Good for nothing except stamping down earth.'

Megan laughed. 'Do you do a lot of that then?'

'Actually, yeah.' Kate looked slightly embarrassed. 'At home, I mean. Gardening and that.'

'Gardening?'

'It's not very interesting,' added Kate hastily. 'To most people.'

'Neither's ballroom dancing,' Megan said with a smile.

Kate smiled back.

'Thanks for the bag.' Megan glanced up at the clock. 'Got to run.'

'Yeah. See you later.'

Megan headed off to registration feeling somewhat more cheerful. *There are other things in the world apart from dancing and Jake*, she told herself sternly. *There are flowers and vegetables.* The thought made her smile.

'What's so funny?' asked Suki.

'Oh, nothing.'

'Tell me.'

'It's nothing, really.'

Suki scowled. 'Is it something about me?'

'About *you*? No, why?'

'It's just that – don't take this the wrong way, Megan, but sometimes you can be quite self-obsessed.'

Megan felt dumbstruck. *Don't take this the wrong way?* How was she *meant* to take it?

Suki saw her expression. 'I don't mean it in a horrible way. It's just that you come across as really secretive. I tell you about things I find funny, don't I?'

'Yes,' replied Megan.

'I pretty much tell you *everything*,' went on Suki. 'That's what friends do. But sometimes you look like you're not even listening!' She saw Megan staring at her. 'What?'

'I've just realized,' said Megan slowly, 'who you remind me of. I can't think why I didn't spot it before.'

'Ooh, who?' Suki looked excited. 'I love these games. Is it someone famous?'

Megan shook her head. 'No. You don't know him.'

'Him?' Suki wrinkled her little nose. 'Are you saying I look like a boy?'

'It's got nothing to do with looks,' Megan said. She almost felt like laughing. How could she not have realized that Suki and Danny were so similar? 'It's the way you are underneath.'

Suki looked uncertain. 'What do you mean?'

Megan came to a decision. 'I'm really sorry,' she said to Suki, 'but I don't think I can be your friend any more.'

Suki's jaw dropped.

'It's just not working,' Megan went on kindly. 'I don't think we have enough in common.'

'You . . .' Suki seemed almost speechless. 'You can't be my *friend*? What is this, *primary school*?' She gave a laugh that sounded forced.

Megan smiled. 'Sorry.' There was no point explaining, she knew. Suki would never understand her point of view. She was incapable of seeing anything outside her own little life – just like Danny.

Suki was starting to look a little panicky. 'Who am I going to sit next to in English?'

'I don't know,' said Megan, 'but I'm sure you'll find someone.'

Suki's eyes narrowed. 'That's it, isn't it?'

'What?'

'You've found another friend already, haven't you? That's why you're dumping me!'

Megan did laugh out loud at this. 'You sound like we're going out together, Suki. No, I haven't found another friend – and actually it's none of your business. I just don't want to hang around with you any more.'

'You'd rather be on your own than with me?' Suki was astounded.

Megan thought for a moment. 'Yes. I would.' The encounter with Kate in the canteen had cheered her up. She smiled. 'See you around.'

'Not if I see you first,' Suki said, turning her back.

♥

'Sounds like you did the right thing,' Jake commented.

'Yeah. She didn't like it though.'

'You're better off without her. And Danny.'

Megan waved a hand at the wall. 'I am totally over him,' she said airily.

'I know when you're lying, Meg.' Jake sounded as though he were smiling. 'It's all right. You don't have to be over him already. He sounded kind of exciting.'

'I don't want exciting,' said Megan firmly. 'I want safe and nice and – and interested in dancing.'

'Well,' said Jake slowly, 'I guess you'll have to look around for someone like that then.'

Megan swallowed. Her heart had just given an extra-hard thump. *Someone like you*, she was on the point of saying, but she clamped her mouth shut. She mustn't blurt it out!

There was an uncomfortable pause. 'Um . . .' said Jake.

'Er . . .' said Megan.

Then they both spoke at once. 'So how's Milton Park?' asked Megan, just as Jake said, 'You'll never believe it but . . .'

They both stopped. 'Sorry, after you.'

'No, you first.'

All of a sudden, both of them seemed completely tongue-tied. It was awful! Megan was terrified that if she started talking, she'd end up blurting out all her feelings, and that would quite possibly be the worst mistake she'd ever made. She couldn't just say, 'Do you fancy me?' could she? What would she do if he said 'No'?

What would she do if he said *'Yes'*?

But Jake didn't seem too comfortable either. He launched into a rapid story about his mum and then got de-railed into a different story about the new shopping centre. His words tumbled over themselves, as though he were frightened of leaving any gaps. Megan found herself saying 'Yeah', 'No' and 'Really?' alternately, with no idea of what she was responding to.

Megan was relieved when her mum called up that dinner was ready. Jake also seemed relieved, as though he couldn't wait to get off the phone. Their goodbyes were so short, Megan had already hung up by the time Jake had got to 'See you.'

She put her head in her hands. Questioning her feelings about Jake had made everything worse, even though she hadn't said anything! Had he guessed? Why was he being weird with her too?

Megan hardly dared to think that perhaps Jake was also wondering about his feelings . . .

♥

Ever since the confrontation with Danny, Megan had avoided walking past the skate park. Instead, she took a more round-about way to reach the arts centre and the shops. But one Tuesday she was running late for salsa, and there just wasn't a choice. Hoping Danny wouldn't be there – or that if he was, he wouldn't see her – she dashed round the corner of the park.

Of course, she couldn't resist glancing across to see if he was there – and immediately wished she hadn't, because Danny just happened to glance up at exactly the same moment. The stormy grey gaze slammed into hers and Megan felt a lump rise in her throat. She had forgotten how good-looking he was! But the stare he was giving her wasn't a friendly one, and she quickly looked away and hurried past.

Rounding the corner, Megan stopped to catch her breath. How could one brief sighting make her feel so wobbly?

'You OK, Megan?' It was Mari, on her way into the centre. 'You look all white.'

'Yeah.' Megan drew a shaky breath. 'Just saw – you know.'

'Ohhh.' Mari nodded in understanding. 'The skate park. Of course.'

'I shouldn't let it bother me,' Megan said crossly. 'I mean, I haven't spoken to him for weeks now, but . . .'

'Come on.' Mari put her arm around Megan's shoulders. 'Let's get to salsa and then you don't have to think about it.'

Corinne was looking anxious when they arrived. 'Oh, thank goodness you're here, Megan. I was beginning to think you weren't coming.'

'Sorry we're late.'

'It's fine – but I want you to take the whole of this lesson to perfect the jive.'

Megan looked surprised. 'Are you sure?'

'Definitely. The salsa is coming along really nicely and it's so free-flowing it doesn't matter if it's not precise. But the party's a week on Saturday and the jive isn't anywhere near perfect yet.' Corinne looked contrite. 'I probably haven't given you enough time to practise in class, Megan. Sorry, I didn't realize how big a task it would be.'

Megan smiled. 'I've been enjoying it, Corinne.'

'Don't worry, she'll lick us into shape,' Mari put in. 'Won't you, Megan?'

'You bet! Right, let's get warmed up.'

'Yes, sir!' Mari saluted.

Corinne sat at the side and watched as Megan took charge. 'The kicks and flicks need to be a lot sharper, everyone, so let's do some of those as a warm up. Remember it's all about control.'

Within minutes, the girls were puffing and panting. 'How come you haven't even broken a sweat yet?' grumbled Jackie.

Megan grinned. 'Years of practice, Jackie.'

'Show-off.'

'And that's another thing,' said Megan, raising her voice, 'you're *supposed* to show off when you do this. It's not like ballet where you need to be all serene and graceful. This needs lots of *energy*! Laugh, whoop, sing along to the music!'

'*Sing along?*' gasped Mari, holding her sides. 'I can barely breathe, let alone sing!'

'Let's take it from the top,' Megan called. She switched on her iPod and the beat started to thump out of the speakers. The girls quickly took up opening positions.

'And a *one*! Two! Three, four, five!' shouted Megan, as the routine began. 'Other way, Alys! Mari, right foot first! And into the kick sequence. *Bounce!*'

Corinne nodded, satisfied, from her position on the floor. The dance was starting to take shape now. Megan had done a good job on the choreography. And the girls really listened to her. She had a natural gift for teaching.

'Is it that time already?' Megan said, when Corinne pointed to the clock. 'But we haven't even got to the end of the routine!'

'I know,' said Corinne, 'but the class is over, Megan.' She got to her feet and looked around at the girls, all of whom were bright red in the face and panting like puppies. 'Do you think there's any chance you could meet another time? It would have to be without me, but you don't need me for this number anyway.'

'We definitely need more time on this,' wheezed Mari. 'And I need a lung transplant.'

Several of the other girls put up their hands. 'Me too.'

'Well,' said Megan doubtfully, 'maybe I've made the routine too hard . . .'

A chorus of 'No's greeted her words. Alys shook her head vigorously. 'No way. It's a brilliant routine.'

'We just need more practice,' agreed Jackie. 'We can put in the time.'

Megan felt a warmth spread through her. They loved her routine! They *wanted* to spend more time working on it! 'Thanks, guys,' she said. 'I really appreciate it.'

'What are we going to wear?' asked Mari suddenly,

going off at a tangent. 'We need jive skirts, like on *Strictly Come Dancing*.'

Corinne smiled. 'That sounds nice. I just thought you could wear something swishy rather than a costume as such.'

Mari pouted. 'I don't have anything swishy. And I think it would be cool if we all wore the same kind of thing.'

'I would ask Candy but she's snowed under with a college production,' said Corinne apologetically. 'And I only have ballet costumes in store, nothing like they wear in ballroom. But we could order outfits from a dancewear company.'

Mari looked unenthusiastic. 'They'll be really expensive, won't they? And we want something specially for *us*.'

'Could we make some skirts?' wondered Alys. 'Nothing fancy, just all matching.'

There was a chorus of groans. 'I can't sew,' said Mari firmly.

'Nor me.'

'Me neither.'

'My mum's really good at sewing,' said Megan before she could stop herself. All eyes swung to her.

'Fantastic!' Mari beamed. 'Thank goodness for that. We can give her money for the fabric.'

'That's great news,' said Corinne, 'but you need to ask her first, Megan. Before everyone gets carried away.'

Megan nodded, wondering what Nicola would say. She had a horrible feeling her mother wouldn't be pleased!

'We haven't sorted out the extra practices, girls,' Alys pointed out. 'Where and when?'

'I've got a huge double garage at home,' offered Jackie. 'I can get my parents to leave the cars out. That's loads of room.'

'I can do Wednesdays and Fridays.'

'I can't do Fridays.'

'Can anyone else do Thursdays?'

'I've got Guides between six and eight.'

'Can we meet after supper?'

'What about homework?'

'What do you want us to do, Megan?'

Megan looked helplessly at Corinne, but Corinne simply held up her hands. 'Now you see how difficult it is being the teacher!'

♥

'You did *WHAT*?' Nicola stared at her daughter. 'You volunteered me to make *thirteen* jive skirts?'

'Sorry.'

Nicola shook her head in stupefaction. 'Your party thing is less than two weeks away!'

'They don't have to be fancy,' Megan tried. 'I've been thinking about it. If I cut out all the pieces – we need them to be circular – then you could just sew them together.'

'Oh, just sew them together. That'll make a lot less work, thanks, Megan,' Nicola said sarcastically.

Megan felt bad. 'I'm sorry. I should have asked you first. Look, I'll tell the girls we'll have to think of something else. They could wear their own skirts. I mean, they wouldn't be quite right, because you need the full circle for the jive, but it'd do. It's only a party, after all . . .'

Nicola suddenly laughed. 'Oh dear, Megan. Your little face. You look so disappointed. All right, I'll help you out. Bless you, you haven't asked for much since we moved here. And I know how much you miss your dancing. I just wish you'd given me a bit more notice.'

Megan smiled, abashed. 'Sorry.'

'Have you got the fabric?'

'No, I thought maybe we could go and choose it after school tomorrow.' Megan looked at her mother hopefully. 'Something shiny? Or glittery? The girls are happy to pay for their share.'

Nicola nodded. 'All right. We'll have to bring Owen though. Don't let him see the Thomas the Tank Engine fabric.'

♥

'This is gorgeous!' Mari twirled around the garage, admiring the silver sequins sprinkled over the black fabric. 'Perfect! Your mum is so clever!'

The other girls crowded round, making admiring noises. 'It swirls out and everything too,' said Alys, fingering the hem. 'How do you make it do that?'

'By making it a full circle,' Megan told her. 'It's got twice as much material in it as a normal skirt. Bit fiddly though.' She didn't mention the blister she had from cutting out pieces for thirteen skirts.

'How can you make sure they'll all fit us?' wondered Jackie. 'I mean, we're not all the same size.'

'Elasticated waists,' replied Megan. 'Practical but not very pretty. Mum suggests that we wear different coloured T-shirts with a belt over the top to hide the waist band. That'll help to make them individual too, because we'll all have different colours.'

'Brilliant.'

'And some of the skirts will be slightly longer because some people are taller than others too. Just make sure you pick the right one. Mum says she hopes to have them all done by next Tuesday.'

'That's only four days before the party,' said Jackie.

Megan nodded. 'I know. But we're working as fast as we can.'

'Well, I think we all owe your mum a huge thank you,' said Alys.

'You owe her more than that,' Megan said with a smirk. 'You each owe her nine pounds twenty-six pence.'

'A bargain,' declared Mari, still twirling around. 'Can I keep it on while we practise today, Megan?'

Megan laughed. 'Of course. Just don't rip it or anything.'

Mari looked hurt. 'I can't believe you'd think that.' She paused for a moment. 'Actually, maybe I had better take it off after all.'

The girls were willing but Megan still found it exhausting trying to get them all to listen to her. When she was working out one section with a couple of girls, the others all started gossiping. And when she told them to be quiet, the ones she had been working with started chatting too!

'Shut up, everyone!' Mari shouted eventually. 'I think Megan is going to explode!'

'Thanks, Mari,' Megan said gratefully. 'It's just that this is taking twice as long as it needs to because people aren't listening.'

The girls looked ashamed. 'Sorry, Megan.'

'It's nearly half-past nine,' Megan pointed out, 'and my dad's coming to pick me up soon. And we've only got one more chance to practise before the party. Not everyone knows all the steps yet, and we can't polish it until we're up to speed. So we need to run it a couple more times.'

'And that means no more talking,' added Mari, wagging her finger at the rest of the girls.

'Especially from you, Mari,' Megan commented with a smile.

Mari pretended to look amazed. 'Talking? Moi?'

'From the top, everyone!' They ran the routine once more and Megan smiled. 'That's better.'

'I wish you had a chance to do more in it,' Mari said, panting. 'You're missing out on all the fun.'

'I can't be in it and watch it at the same time,' Megan said, though she felt a twinge at Mari's words. She did love the jive. 'Besides, there's an odd number with me. It makes sense for me to start off the routine and then duck out so you can do the paired stuff.'

'But you're the best!' remarked Mari. 'It's crazy that you don't get a chance to show what you can do.'

'You should be doing a solo,' Alys suggested.

Megan laughed. 'No thank you. There's no time to choreograph anything else. And besides, I'm used to dancing with a partner.'

'Well, maybe that's not so impossible—' Mari started to say, but she was interrupted by a knock on the garage door.

'Someone's mum is early,' commented Jackie, but it wasn't a parent.

'Sean!' Mari exclaimed, as the door went up to reveal a tall red-headed boy. He looked a bit taken aback by the group of girls.

'Oh – er, sorry. I was looking for Mari.'

'You're early,' Mari told him, blushing furiously, much to everyone's amusement. 'We're still rehearsing. Go away and come back in twenty minutes.'

'You can't tell him to do that!' Megan said, astonished. 'It's dark outside and it's freezing.' She turned to Sean and smiled. 'Hi, Sean. I'm Megan. Come in and watch, if you like. We could do with an audience and we were just about to run it again.'

'No, it's OK,' said Sean, shooting a sideways glance at Mari. 'I don't want to get in the way.'

'Don't be silly.' Megan grabbed his arm and pulled

him into the garage. 'Besides, you're letting in a draught.'

'Why did you do that?' Mari hissed at her as Megan closed the garage door and the girls got into their opening positions again. 'I don't want him watching!'

'You can't leave him out in the cold,' Megan whispered back in a reasonable voice. 'And what's the difference? He'll see it next week anyway, won't he?' She looked hard at Mari's face. 'You *did* invite him, didn't you?'

'Um . . .'

'Oh, *Mari*. Go and take up position. We'll have to talk later.'

Sean clapped loudly at the end. 'That was fantastic,' he said. 'You're all really good.'

'Except me,' said Mari in a mocking tone.

Sean stared at her. 'You were really good too, Mari.'

Mari blushed, pleased but embarrassed.

'I think that's enough for tonight,' Megan said. 'It's getting there. If we can meet once more next week, I think we're going to nail it.'

The girls started to gather up their things. Jackie opened the garage doors and they trooped out one by one. 'Thanks, Megan,' said Alys. 'I nearly got every single step right that time. You're really patient.'

'You're doing so well,' Megan told her. 'Just keep

concentrating, but try not to look as though you are, if you know what I mean.'

Alys waved. 'See you next week at salsa.'

Soon there was only Mari, Sean, Megan and Jackie left in the garage. Jackie was hunting around for the garage door keys. 'I'm sure I put them down here,' she muttered. 'My dad'll kill me if I've lost them.'

Megan glanced over to the other two. 'I had no idea you were so good at dancing,' Sean was saying to Mari.

Mari looked uncomfortable. 'I'm not really.'

Sean gave a laugh. 'Are you kidding? That was amazing! I thought you said you had no rhythm.'

'I don't.'

'Mari . . .'

She gave him a playful shove. 'Stop flattering me. You know I don't like it.'

Megan caught the look of frustration on Sean's face and felt sorry for him. 'You *are* good, Mari,' she said, moving over to join them. 'You should stop putting yourself down.'

'That's what I keep telling her,' he said, with a rueful grin. 'But she won't listen to me.'

'That's because you're an idiot,' said Mari, jokingly.

Megan grimaced on Sean's behalf. How could Mari talk to him like that when he was clearly so fond of her? A car beeped outside. 'I should be off. Think that's my dad's car out there.'

'Found them!' Jackie stood up, dishevelled but happy, brandishing a keyring.

'Thanks for lending us your garage,' Mari said. She turned back to Megan. 'And please thank your mum for the skirts, Megan. They're going to look amazing.'

'I will.' Megan smiled at Sean. 'Nice to meet you.'

He grinned back, his whole face lit up with the smile. 'You too. Mari says you're a bit of a dance diva.'

'In a *good* way,' Mari said hurriedly.

Sean's expression was comical. 'Oh God, yes. Not diva like being all stroppy. I meant diva like goddess-type thing.'

Megan laughed. It seemed Sean had the same ability to put his foot in it as Mari. Which only made them even better matched, surely.

She wondered why Mari didn't make the most of what she'd got. Sean wasn't going anywhere, was he? So why was Mari still keeping him at arm's length?

Chapter 17

I think I made a bit of a mistake

'Hair up or hair down?' wondered Mari, standing in front of Megan's mirror and holding her hair in a makeshift ponytail. 'See, I think up is better for the jive, but down is better for the salsa.'

Megan laughed. 'I don't think it really matters, Mari. And it's not as though we've got different costumes for the salsa and the jive. This isn't a competition.'

'I know,' said Mari, 'but I'm still excited. It's like being in a play, only scarier.'

'Is your friend Fliss coming?'

'No, she can't. But Victoria said she might be there.' Mari grinned. 'Can't wait to see the look on her face. She'll never believe what I've been doing.'

'Maybe you could talk her into joining the class next term,' suggested Megan, trying to apply mascara without poking herself in the eye.

'I'll try,' said Mari, 'but I know what she'll say. It's not really her thing.'

'It wasn't yours either to start with,' Megan pointed out.

'True!' Mari made a decision and started to pull her hair into a high ponytail.

'I think I'll wear mine up too,' said Megan, doing up her belt. 'Then it won't get in the way. We're doing salsa first, right?'

'Yup. Corinne said we should because it's a salsa class. So salsa first, then she does a little speech thing, then there's drinks and nibbles and some free dancing, then jive about an hour later, then everyone dances again and we all say merry Christmas.' Mari giggled. 'Sean was worried we were going to play salsa music all evening, but I told him there'd be some disco stuff too.'

'You invited him then?' Megan tried not to sound too interested.

Mari shrugged. 'Had to, didn't I, after he saw our practice? I'd told him it was for some in-class thing, but he kept on saying he wanted to come along and watch one day. I was terrified he'd just turn up at class, so I told him about the party. I really thought he wouldn't be interested but he said he was up for a laugh. So he's coming.'

'That's great!'

'Yeah, well he's an even worse dancer than I am, so

maybe having him there will make me look good.'
Mari caught the expression on Megan's face. 'Uh-oh.
Go on, then.'

'What?'

'You're dying to say something, I can tell. Go on,
spit it out.'

Megan took a breath. 'Well, I don't want to inter-
fere. And it's really none of my business.'

Mari laughed. 'We're friends, Megan. You can tell
me.'

'All right. But don't be mad at me. It's only that . . .
I wondered . . . why you're so mean to him all the
time?'

Mari's eyes opened wide. 'Mean to him? What are
you talking about?'

'Well, you put him down all the time,' said Megan,
wondering just how honest she could be. Even though
Mari had said it was OK, she didn't want to upset
her. 'When I asked you what he was like, you said he
wasn't very good-looking.'

'He's not!'

'I'm not sure I agree with you,' Megan said slowly.
'I mean, he's not drop-dead-gorgeous. Not in a traditional kind of way. But when he smiles, it's like he's all
warm and comforting. Don't you think?'

'He is a bit,' admitted Mari. 'Like a cosy blanket.'

'And that sort of makes him good-looking, as far as I'm concerned,' said Megan.

'Hmm,' said Mari, staring at herself in the mirror. 'I suppose you've got a point.'

'Do you like him, Mari?'

'Of course I do.'

'Then how come you don't tell him?' Megan pressed.

Mari sighed. 'We've been through this, Megan. I don't want him to get the wrong idea. I don't know how I feel about *myself* half the time, let alone him.'

'But you can tell him that too,' Megan suggested. 'If he cares about you, then he won't mind if sometimes you're a bit unsure.'

Mari bit her lip. 'If I tell you something, you promise you won't tell anyone else?'

'Of course.'

Mari looked down at the floor. 'I don't understand why he likes me. When I'm – I'm fat.'

'*What?*' Megan's mouth dropped open. 'What are you talking about? You are *not* fat!'

'My mum says I am,' Mari said miserably.

'Your mum's wrong.'

'But I'm not skinny like you,' Mari pointed out. 'Boys are supposed to like skinny girls, aren't they? Like all the ones in the magazines.'

'Sean likes *you*,' said Megan. She couldn't believe she was hearing this. Confident, bubbly, loud Mari was really insecure about her looks!

'But *why*?' wailed Mari.

'Because you're funny,' Megan said, taking her hand. 'You're *hilarious*. And you care about stuff. You've worked so hard at this dancing, when it hasn't come easily. You don't give up. You're a cheerful sort of person; people like being around you because you make them feel better. And from what I've seen, Sean is the same sort of person. I think you're a perfect match.'

Mari pulled a face. 'How come you're the expert all of a sudden?'

Megan let go of Mari's hand. 'I've been doing a lot of thinking lately,' she confessed. 'That thing with Danny – it opened my eyes. I got a bit swept away by him. But it made me think about what I should look for in a boyfriend. What any girl should look for.'

'And what have you decided?' Mari was looking less miserable.

'Well,' said Megan, suddenly feeling rather embarrassed, 'I think he should be kind. That's the most important thing.'

'Kind to you?'

'Kind to everyone. I don't want someone who keeps

getting into trouble because he's rude. I don't want to have to apologize for him upsetting people.'

Mari nodded. 'Sounds good. So, item one: helps little old ladies across the street and buys you flowers.'

Megan laughed. 'You're not taking this very seriously, Mari.'

'Sorry, sorry. Go on. I'm all ears.' Mari put her hands behind her ears and pushed them forward. 'See?'

'I'm going to ignore that,' Megan told her, trying not to smile. 'OK then. Secondly, he needs to like things I enjoy doing. And I need to like things he enjoys doing too. I mean, we need to be prepared to try out new stuff.'

'I thought that was the problem with Danny,' Mari commented. 'You tried out all this new stuff and didn't like it.'

'I *did* like it,' objected Megan. 'But he didn't enjoy anything *I* loved. I mean, remember the time I took him to the theatre? He didn't even *try* to like it. I see that now.'

'OK. So, item two: common interests. You have to enjoy doing stuff together.'

'And I also think,' said Megan slowly, 'that you have to feel completely comfortable talking to him. He has to be a good listener.'

Mari rolled her eyes. 'You're starting to sound

like a magazine. Top Ten Things to Look For in a Boyfriend.'

'But it's really important,' insisted Megan. 'Danny never really listened to me. He didn't ask me questions about myself. He talked about himself all the time. And if I told him anything, he was always thinking about something else.'

'Remind me why you went out with him again?' Mari stuck out her tongue.

Megan laughed. 'You're right. I have no idea. Swept away, I guess. And I was a bit lonely.'

'Missing Jake?' Mari raised her eyebrows.

Megan looked down at her hands. 'Maybe a bit, yeah. And now here's something *you* can't tell anyone else. Mari, I think I made a bit of a mistake.'

'With Jake?'

Megan got off the bed and checked her make-up in the mirror so that she didn't have to look at Mari. There was a hot feeling in her stomach. 'I think maybe you guys were right. He . . . we might have been perfect together.' She blushed. 'I haven't stopped thinking about him for the past two weeks. Which is stupid, isn't it? I mean, it's too late. I can't go out with someone who lives so far away. And he probably doesn't feel that way about me. I mean, he's never – we've never . . . *I* never thought about him like that until recently. *He* probably still thinks of me as a friend. And it's not something you can ask someone over the phone. So it's crazy even thinking about it – I mean, when are we actually likely to be face to face again?'

Mari opened her mouth and then closed it again.

'What?' The hot feeling was making it hard to breathe. Megan couldn't quite believe she'd said it out loud. Would Mari tell her it was all pointless?

'Oh, nothing,' Mari said, but her eyes looked strangely excited. 'I was just thinking . . . what would you say to him? If you saw him, I mean?'

'It doesn't matter,' replied Megan. 'He lives in York-shire. It wouldn't work.'

'But if you had the opportunity,' persisted Mari, leaning forward. 'What would you tell him?'

'I don't know. What I just told you, I guess. That I wished we'd had a chance to go out together – like on a date. Not a dance class, or a competition, or at school. That he's always been my best friend, and it wasn't until I moved away that I started to think that maybe he meant more to me than that.' Megan shook her head. 'Oh, what's the use? There's no point think-ing about it now.' She glanced at the clock. 'Come on, we're going to be late.'

Mari leaped up. 'I'm really nervous!'

Megan smiled at her fondly. 'You're going to be fine, Mari. It's a real shame your mum can't come. She'd be so excited to see what you can do.'

'She's most excited about the fact that I've lost four pounds.' Mari rolled her eyes. 'Still, at least it means she's keen for me to keep coming to salsa next term.'

Megan smiled. 'That's great, Mari. And you'll have Victoria there to watch you. And Sean, of course. He's going to be gobsmacked!'

'That makes it worse,' said Mari glumly.

'You are impossible!' Megan exclaimed. 'Sean is lovely! He's sweet and kind and interested in you – in fact, all the things I just talked about! *He* doesn't care that you're not a skinny size nothing. He likes you just as you are – and you're just messing him around! Mari, if you're not sure you like him enough, then you should break up with him.'

'Break up?' Mari looked shocked.

'Yes. Don't keep him hanging on like this – it's not fair. Now, have you got everything? Let's go.'

♥

Even from the outside, the hall looked inviting. Purple and silver heart-shaped balloons were blowing in the breeze, attached by curling ribbons to the porch roof.

Fairy lights framed the doorway, twinkling in the dark. Megan felt a little thrill in her stomach.

'This looks lovely,' said Nicola in appreciation. 'Someone must have spent quite a lot of time decorating this.'

Megan and Mari exchanged guilty glances. Jackie and Alys had volunteered to help Corinne with the decorating, but had said eagerly that any other helpers would be most welcome. 'I'm about as artistic as a blind beetle,' Mari had declared. Megan had been about to volunteer when Mari had asked, 'I don't suppose I could get ready at your house, could I? Only my mum has to work and so there'll be no one at home . . .'

Jackie and Alys, whether they'd had extra help or not, had certainly done a fantastic job. As Megan and Mari went into the hall, they gasped. 'Pretty!' cried Owen, running past them and straight into the middle of the room.

Around the edges of the hall were tables and chairs, arranged in groups. At the stage end was a long narrow table already groaning under the weight of the various dishes and plates of food. 'I'll go and add mine,' said Nicola, taking her tray of vegetable lasagne across. More purple and silver balloons decorated the tables and windows, whilst silver tinsel and fairy lights were strung across the beams. And by the door, where they had just come in, stood a large white Christmas tree with silver and purple butterflies pinned to it.

In the centre of the hall, a large area had been left clear for dancing. And above the floor, right in the middle of the ceiling . . . a large, beautiful, glittering mirror ball! Two carefully focused spotlights sent little star-like reflections dancing across the walls and the floor.

'She got it!' breathed Mari, staring up at the mirror ball. 'I can't believe it . . . she actually got it!'

'It's pretty,' said Owen, pointing. 'Look, stars!'

'That's an impressive piece of kit,' said Bryan.

Megan turned to smile at him. 'I'm so glad you could all come.'

He smiled back and tugged her ponytail. 'Wouldn't miss it for the world, chicken. It's you dancing, isn't it?'

As if on cue, someone switched on the sound system, and music came pouring out of the wall-mounted speakers. Corinne, wearing a full-length turquoise dress, came over to meet Bryan and Nicola. 'Your daughter is a great teacher,' she told them. 'Dancer too, yes, but she's managed to get them all doing exactly what she tells them.'

'Gets it from her mother,' said Bryan. Nicola trod on his foot. 'Ow!'

'And I've been very grateful,' Corinne went on, 'because Megan has been a huge help in the class. With all her experience, it's been great.'

Megan blushed as her father squeezed her shoulder.

'Megan is a very good dancer,' Owen told her solemnly.

'I know.' Corinne bent down to him. 'Do you dance too?'

He nodded. 'But only at home.'

'Well, maybe you should think about coming along to one of my classes,' Corinne said, amused. 'I run ballet and tap classes for children your age.'

Owen frowned for a moment. 'I'm not sure,' he said. 'I really want to do breakdancing. Like when you spin on your head.'

Corinne burst out laughing. 'Wow. Well, I'm afraid we don't do that in ballet or tap. But maybe you could start off with something a bit easier than spinning on your head?'

'I'll think about it,' Owen promised. 'If I don't find anything better.'

'Mari.'

Megan and Mari turned to see Sean standing in the

doorway, looking rather awkward. 'Hey,' said Mari. There was a pause.

'You look great,' Megan said, trying to fill the silence. 'You're wearing a tie!'

Sean tugged on the multicoloured tie at his neck. 'Yeah,' he said. 'Thought I should make a bit of an effort, you know. You look really nice, Mari.'

To Megan's intense delight, Mari was blushing. 'Thanks.'

'Uh . . . we're going to get sorted at a table,' Nicola said, tactfully dragging Owen and Bryan away.

'Yeah,' said Megan. 'Um . . . I'll come with you.' She left Mari and Sean standing staring at each other on the dance floor and followed her family over to a table.

'Is that Mari's boyfriend?' Nicola asked in a low voice.

'Yes,' Megan whispered back, 'but it hasn't been going very well.'

'Looks like it's OK now,' commented Nicola, nodding towards the floor, where Sean was shyly taking Mari's hand and leading her over to a table.

'About time,' said Megan, feeling very happy for Mari.

The hall was filling up by the minute, and Megan could see Corinne glancing at her watch. The girls from the salsa class had all arrived now, looking really smart in their jive skirts. Each girl had chosen a plain-coloured top to go with her black skirt, so they were a whole rainbow of colours. Megan was pleased she had chosen a dark green top to wear; she knew it brought out the green in her eyes. 'You girls all look lovely,' said Nicola, following Megan's gaze. 'The skirts have turned out really well.'

'Thanks so much, Mum.' Megan gave her a hug. She glanced over to Mari and Sean and spotted a tall slim girl with beautiful dark skin and long black hair just joining them. Mari squealed and jumped up to hug her. *That must be Victoria*, Megan thought. She felt a lot happier that Mari had friends there to support her.

Corinne waved at Megan from the middle of the dance floor. 'It's time,' Megan said. 'We're going to do the salsa we've been practising.'

'Can I come?' Owen asked.

'Sorry.' Megan bent down. 'It's just the girls from the class to start with. But you can join in afterwards.'

'OK,' said Owen, losing interest. 'I'm hungry anyway.'

Megan and the other girls took up their positions on the dance floor. Some of the parents and friends hadn't noticed what was happening, but as soon as

Corinne turned up the music and hit 'play', they turned round.

It was a traditional salsa tune with a contemporary feel, and Megan felt the music spread up from her toes through her whole body. It was impossible *not* to dance! She threw herself into the moves, and around her she knew the other girls were doing the same. It was amazing to feel part of a synchronized dance group, with their audience only arm's length away!

As ever, the dance felt like it was over in a flash, but the response was immediate. Parents and friends rose to their feet, clapping and cheering. Flushed, Megan took a bow with the other girls and then went back to her table. 'That was great!' Nicola told her, beaming.

Corinne called for attention. 'Good evening! It's lovely to see so many of you here supporting the girls.' The audience quietened down again to listen. 'When I started the salsa class back in September,' Corinne went on, 'I never imagined it would take off so quickly. But the girls have all been so dedicated and enthusiastic, teaching them has been a real pleasure. And it's wonderful that you've all come out on this dark and cold evening to see what they've achieved in such a short space of time. I think you'll agree they've done themselves proud.' She led the applause. 'We're going to have some food and some dancing – and do have a go at some salsa steps yourselves, they're easier than they look! The girls will be happy to show you what to do, I'm sure.' She smiled. 'And then in about an hour, the girls are going to do a completely different dance for you. One of the class – Megan Hirst – has had quite a career in ballroom dancing already.' Megan went bright red. 'And she has been teaching a brand-new dance to the group,' went on Corinne with a grin. 'I won't spoil it for you by telling you what it is – you'll have to wait and see! Oh – and one last thing.' She beckoned to Jackie, who was standing in the shadows holding something. 'We want to say a big thank you to Megan's mum, Nicola, who spent hours making all those beautiful skirts for the girls. These are for you.'

'Oh!' said Nicola, as Jackie presented her with a huge bouquet of flowers. 'How lovely! Thank you so much – honestly, it was a pleasure.'

'Don't say that,' Megan told her, 'otherwise you'll have to make our costumes next time too!'

'Anyway, that's quite enough from me,' said Corinne. 'Please – help yourselves to food, and help yourselves to salsa too!'

The music went back on, and the noise level rose. 'This is just what we need this Christmas,' said Bryan, looking round approvingly. 'All the family at a big party, with good food, dancing and company.'

Megan gave him a hug. 'Thanks, Dad.'

'Me hug too,' Owen said in a babyish voice.

Bryan laughed, and pulled the boy onto his lap. 'You too, Owen. Come on, Nicky.'

'I'll squash my flowers! Hang on a minute.' Nicola laid her bouquet on the table and joined in the cuddle. 'First Christmas in Parchester! Well done, everyone, for coping with the move so well. I feel we've really settled in here.'

'Me too,' agreed Bryan. 'New jobs, new friends, new life!'

Nicola saw Megan pull a face. 'Megan?'

'Oh, I'm all right,' said Megan hastily. 'Honestly. It was hard to start with, but it's a lot better now.'

'Yeah?' Nicola put a hand on her daughter's chin and tilted it up. 'You looked like you were thinking of something in particular.'

Megan shrugged and tried to sound casual. 'I guess I still miss Milton, that's all. And Jake, of course.' She felt her cheeks grow warm and desperately hoped she wasn't blushing too noticeably.

Nicola and Bryan exchanged a look. 'Well,' said Nicola, 'you've been very brave about it all. And who knows, maybe things will turn out for the best.'

Megan was puzzled. 'What are you talking about?'

'I'm *hungry*,' whined Owen. 'The people over there have sausage rolls!'

'Come on, hungry monster.' Nicola got up and took Owen's hand. 'Let's get you some dinner.'

Megan trailed after them, wondering what Nicola had meant. As she stood in the queue for food, she spotted Mari and Sean sitting together with Victoria. The two of them were holding hands under the table. She smiled, but something inside ached and she knew it was because she wanted the same thing for herself. She wanted *Jake's* hand holding hers under the table. The thought made her tingle.

Megan sighed and went to get some food.

♥

It took a while for people to pluck up the courage to dance, but before too long, there were lots of people on the dance floor trying out the salsa steps that Megan and the other girls were teaching them. Mari dragged Victoria over to introduce her to Megan, and Victoria seemed more than willing to have a go at the salsa. 'It would be lovely if you came to class next term,' Megan told her.

Victoria grinned. 'I'll think about it. If Mari can do it then anyone can.'

'Hey!' Mari shoved her affectionately.

It seemed no time at all before Corinne was calling them all together to get ready for the jive.

'I'm not sure I can bounce with all this food inside me,' groaned Jackie.

'I told you not to have second helpings of gateau,' Alys said.

'But there might not be any left afterwards,' Jackie explained. 'Oof!'

Megan grinned at Mari. She was usually the first to join in any conversation about food. But Mari was looking oddly distracted. 'You OK, Mari?' asked Megan.

'Huh? Oh, yeah. Yes, I'm fine.' But Mari's eyes kept flicking to the door.

Megan followed her gaze curiously. 'What are you looking at?'

'Nothing, nothing. Just nervous.' Mari swung round brightly. 'So! Let's do this!'

Corinne beckoned them all close. 'This term has been brilliant,' she told them. 'And you've worked really hard at the salsa. This is your turn – well, yours and Megan's. Give it some real energy – and happy Christmas!'

The girls cheered. 'Yeah!' Alys punched the air. 'Let's go!'

The music started, and within two bars the audience had started clapping along. '*Strickly!*' yelled Owen, bouncing up and down on Bryan's lap. 'Jill and Darren on YouTube! Yeah!'

His father laughed. 'You don't even know who Jill and Darren are!'

'They're dancers!' shouted Owen excitedly.

Megan joined the girls for the opening, and then, as planned, moved to one side so that they could pair up. She watched with a real glow of pride – they were doing so well! Jackie and Alys were kicking and flicking for all they were worth, despite the fact that Jackie had eaten too much. A small mistake caught her eye, and Megan frowned. It wasn't like Mari to go wrong in that part of the dance. And now she was on the wrong foot! It looked like she wasn't concentrating at all!

Megan waited for her cue and ran in to join the final bars of the song. It came to a rousing finish, and the girls struck the final position. Again, the audience rose to their feet, clapping and cheering even louder than they had for the salsa. Megan felt flushed with pride. Her first group choreography! And it had gone really well. She saw her family clapping and beaming at her, and Owen so excited he was running round and round in circles. She saw Corinne clapping and smiling, Victoria trying to blow a wolf whistle, and Sean, who was whooping and punching his fist in the air. Megan smiled. *He* wouldn't mind that Mari made a mistake or two! She wondered what had distracted Mari – had she been looking at the doorway again?

Automatically, Megan's own eyes swung round – and for a moment, the world whirled into darkness and her knees felt weak.

Standing in the doorway, clapping and smiling at her, was Jake.

Chapter 18

surprise!

Megan felt rooted to the spot. Suddenly Mari was at her elbow. 'Surprise!' she whispered.

Megan couldn't take her eyes off Jake. 'Is he – how did you . . . ?'

'Nicked the number from your mobile,' grinned Mari. 'When we went out to dinner. I've been ringing him on and off ever since, trying to get this organized. You wouldn't believe how difficult it's been – and I've nearly blabbed it all several times!' She nudged Megan in the back. 'Aren't you going over then?'

As though in a dream, Megan moved towards the doorway, and Jake came towards her. How could she have forgotten how good-looking he was? True, he may not have defined cheekbones and model looks, but there was something so *warm* about him. The expression in his eyes, the way his hair still stuck up on top of his head – she loved all those things about him, didn't she? How could she ever have thought

Danny so good-looking? Next to Jake, Danny's looks seemed false and superficial.

'Hi,' he said.

'Hi.'

They were only a couple of feet apart, but Megan suddenly couldn't think of anything to say. And to her intense embarrassment she was blushing!

'That was great,' said Jake, indicating the dance floor. 'That jive. Is that the one you choreographed?'

Megan was unable to do anything but nod. *This is ridiculous!* she told herself. *Pull yourself together – it's just Jake!* 'Um – wow. It's amazing to see you. What are you doing here?'

'Came to see you, of course.' Jake grinned. 'Heard you were having a party, and you didn't invite me.' His gaze flicked over her shoulder. 'Your friend Mari's a bit mad, isn't she? Been texting me every day the last week to make sure I was still coming!'

Megan laughed. 'That sounds like her, yes.' She turned to glance over her shoulder and caught Mari's eye. Mari immediately turned away and pretended to be talking to someone else.

'Besides,' Jake went on, 'I wanted to check up on your dancing. Can't have your standards slipping, can we?'

'There's no ballroom round here,' Megan pointed

out. 'There aren't any classes for me to go to except this one.'

'Actually . . .' Corinne suddenly appeared at her shoulder. 'I've been making some enquiries about that. And I think I might have found someone. So don't worry too much, Megan. I think you might be able to get back to real training after Christmas. I'll let your parents know.' She drifted away again.

Megan raised her eyebrows, stunned. 'Wow. That came out of nowhere. This is an evening of surprises.'

'Yeah.' Jake reached out and took her hand. 'Um . . . can you take another one?'

Megan's heart suddenly seemed to be beating twice as fast. 'What kind of surprise?'

'Well . . .' Jake glanced over at Mari again. 'Mari was wondering whether you and I would do a dance together. She said she'd asked Corinne if it would be all right. For old times' sake.'

'What sort of dance?'

Jake smiled. 'What do you think? Our waltz, of course. Our competition winner.'

'But . . .' Megan withdrew her hand in panic. 'But I haven't done it since the summer! I can't even remember it!'

'Course you can,' Jake told her. 'We practised it every day for months. It'll come back.'

Megan's throat went dry. 'I haven't got my dress,' she said helplessly. 'My waltz dress.'

Jake looked across at her family. 'I think your mum brought it.'

'*What?*' Megan's head snapped round. 'They *knew*? They *knew* about this?'

'Don't get mad,' Jake begged. 'They had to be in on it. Besides, my stepdad . . . oh God. You're not annoyed I'm here, are you?' His face fell. 'This isn't the biggest mistake ever, is it?' He lowered his voice. 'Are you still – I mean – do you wish I was Danny? I know you wanted him to come.'

'*What?* Of course not! Why would I want him here after the way he treated me?'

'So why are you angry?' Jake looked anxious. 'Do you want me to go away again?'

On an impulse, Megan put out her hand to grab his arm. The contact sent a tingle through her fingers. 'No, don't! Of course I don't want you to go away again. I'm just a bit shocked, that's all. And to think you've all been planning this behind my back . . .'

Jake took her hand and squeezed it. 'But it's a *good* surprise, right?'

Megan looked into his eyes and her heart beat faster.

It was almost as though she were seeing him for the first time. Why had she never realized how she felt before? She swallowed. 'It's a *really* good surprise.'

Jake smiled and his gaze softened. 'You look great, Megan. It's so good to see you.'

Megan just nodded, not trusting her voice. He'd never looked at her in quite that way before . . .

'So are you OK to do our waltz?'

Megan pulled back her hand, trying to compose herself. 'For old times' sake?' she said lightly.

'Exactly. And . . . sort of for new times' sake too.'

'Pardon?'

Jake looked a little worried. 'I've sort of got another surprise. It's a good one though, I hope.'

'What's going on?'

'Well, it's not quite definite yet . . .'

'What do you mean, it's not definite? What are you talking about?'

'Stephen's got an interview,' said Jake. 'On Monday. In Parchester. With your dad's company.'

'In . . .' Words failed Megan. Automatically she glanced towards her family. Her father smiled broadly at her and gave her a thumbs-up. 'You mean your stepdad might be working here?'

'Like I said, we don't know yet. But the company asked him to come for interview. They actually headhunted Stephen! So they really want him to come and work for them. I think someone's leaving or retiring and your dad put in a good word.'

Megan shook her head. 'I can't take this in . . . what are you saying?'

Jake took a breath. 'We might be coming to live here.'

'Oh my God! Really?' Megan felt a huge smile spread across her face.

Jake grinned in relief. 'You'd be pleased about that?'

'*Pleased?* You don't know *how* pleased!'

'I wasn't sure . . . Now that you've got new friends and everything.'

'Oh, don't be daft!'

Mari bounced over. 'I couldn't wait any longer! Are you guys going to dance for us or what?'

Megan looked at Jake. 'I guess we are,' she said.

Mari let out a scream. 'This is so perfect! I knew it! Megan, your mum brought your dress.' She thrust out a bag. 'It might be a bit crumpled but we couldn't risk you seeing it. Sorry about the top secret stuff, by the way. I just thought it would be so cool if you didn't know!' She looked anxious for a moment. 'You didn't guess, did you?'

'No,' said Megan, laughing. 'I didn't guess.'

'I knew it!' Mari squeaked again. 'Quickly then, go get dressed!'

'What about you? Did you bring your suit?' Megan turned to Jake, who grinned.

'Got it on under my coat.'

♥

As soon as the music started, Megan knew she would remember all the steps. It was as though the combination of Jake, her costume and the so-familiar music had unlocked that secret part of her that had hidden the memory away. As the first notes of 'It Is You I Have Loved All Along' floated out of the speakers, she felt her body focus itself to the music. Dressed again in the floor-length white ballgown that she loved so much, it was as though the previous few months were melting away. Nicola had spent many late evenings painstakingly sewing the tiny silver sequins onto the taffeta skirt, and there were little diamantés in spiral shapes all over the white satin bodice. A simple tiara perched on her head and Megan felt every inch the fairytale princess of the song. She smiled at her fairytale prince, who was standing opposite and gazing at her as though no one else in the room existed.

The room fell silent around them as Megan stepped into Jake's arms and they began to glide around the floor. The slowly twirling mirror ball added a dream-like quality, and it seemed to Megan as though they were drifting through a starry night sky. It felt so right; so perfect that she was back in Jake's arms, her body mirroring the moves he made, so that they were almost one with the music.

How could she ever have thought that dancing wasn't as exciting as racing? It was better than that – it was like *flying*! All those times with Danny – the skateboarding, the go-karts, the BMX riding – it all felt completely unreal, as though it didn't matter at all. *This* was what she loved, wasn't it? This – dancing her favourite dance of all time, with Jake – her perfect partner. Beside Jake, the memory of Danny simply evaporated in a puff of Christmas mist.

And as Megan effortlessly moved across the floor, it was as though she were hearing the words of the song for the very first time. How Jake and she had laughed over its sentimentality when they first heard it! But neither of them was laughing now. The lyrics talked of mysteries dissolved; of every-thing becoming clear. 'It is you I have loved all along.' And Megan looked into Jake's eyes as the song came to an end and wondered if he could see right into her heart and how it was singing for him.

The applause was immediate, and if Megan had looked round, she would have seen her mother wiping her eyes and Mari squeezing Sean's hand so hard that his knuckles were white. But she only had eyes for Jake.

And Jake glanced up at the mirror ball and smiled. 'Have you seen what else is up there?'

Megan followed his gaze and saw, almost hidden in the shadows, a tiny bunch of mistletoe tied to the beam with a silver ribbon. 'Oh. I suppose that means . . .'

He looked at her again. 'I suppose it does. If you want to, that is . . .'

'Well . . . maybe just this once . . .'

She closed her eyes as he leaned towards her.

'Just once, Meg?' Jake whispered. 'Because there's something else I need to tell you . . . about how I feel . . . Can you take one more surprise?'

THE END

You can meet some of the Sweet Hearts girls again
in the brand-new book

Ice
Dreams

Available soon

Read on to find out who . . .

At 9.25 a.m. on Saturday, Tania was standing nervously outside the Playhouse Stage Door. She had brought everything she could possibly need for the day – dance wear, ballet shoes, packed lunch, water bottle, hairbrush . . .

'Could you not find a bigger bag?' said Zac, eyeing the enormous shoulder bag.

'How did you manage to fit everything into *that*?' asked Tania, prodding Zac's empty-looking rucksack.

He shrugged. 'Leotard, tights, shoes. What else would I need?'

Tania smirked. 'Where did you get them?'

'Borrowed them,' said Zac shortly, and Tania was delighted to see a slight flush to his cheeks. 'Didn't think they'd let me in without them.'

'Speaking of which,' said Tania, 'we'd better go in.'

The Stage Door manager directed them to a rehearsal room on the first floor, and Tania and Zac were surprised to see several other young people limbering up outside. 'I thought this was just for us,' whispered Zac.

One of the girls, clad in an all-in-one peacock-coloured leotard, looked up. 'It's a general workshop,' she said. 'Didn't you read the leaflet?'

'We didn't arrange it,' said Tania hastily. 'Someone else did.'

'You were lucky,' said the peacock girl. 'Places got snapped up really quickly. They are the Ballet Formidable, after all.' She said this in such an impressed tone of voice that Zac and Tania exchanged glances.

'Wonder how Brock managed to wangle this one?' murmured Zac.

'We'd better get changed.'

'Girls' changing is down there.' The peacock girl pointed. 'Boys' is on the next floor up.'

'See you in a minute,' said Zac, and ran lightly up the stairs.

The peacock girl followed Tania into the changing rooms and went straight to a bag hanging on a peg. 'He's cute,' she said casually, fishing out a hairbrush, even though her hair was already immaculate. 'He your boyfriend?'

'No,' said Tania shortly. 'He – um – we skate together.'

'What, like inlining?'

'No, ice skating.'

The peacock girl sat down on the bench. 'I'm Suki,' she said, 'by the way.'

'Tania.'

'Ice skating, wow,' said Suki. 'I always wanted to do ice skating but my ballet teacher said it would be bad for my knees.'

Tania swiftly got out of her outdoor clothes and wriggled into her tights. 'Bad for your knees? I never heard that before.'

Suki shrugged. 'My teacher used to be professional. With the Birmingham Royal Ballet. She would know.'

Tania kept quiet. She was sure Suki would be quite happy to provide most of the conversation.

After patting her hair ineffectively, Suki put her hairbrush back in her bag and reached for a pot of lip gloss. 'So if you're an ice skater, what are you doing here?'

'My coach booked the workshop,' said Tania.

'Oh, right. Because my friend wanted to come but she was told there weren't any more places. And this was weeks ago.'

'Oh dear.' Tania didn't dare mention that Brock had only booked the class a couple of days previously.

'We're both going to the Rambert open workshop next week,' said Suki. 'My friend and me. My teacher says they look out for potential new members at the workshops.'

'Oh, do they?' Tania flicked her leotard straps over her shoulders, wishing Suki would go away.

'But of course I'd rather join the Bolshoi,' said Suki. 'Or the Royal.'

'Don't you have to train at the Royal Ballet School for that?'

Suki shot her a look of pure venom. 'Some people don't mature until later,' she said coldly.

'Pardon?' Tania was baffled.

'I didn't get a place at eleven,' said Suki, as if the words tasted nasty in her mouth. 'But it wasn't my fault.'

'Oh.'

Suki looked Tania up and down. 'Is that what you're wearing?'

Tania glanced down at her pale pink tights, plum-coloured leotard, warm-up leggings and leather ballet shoes. 'Yes, why?'

'No reason.' Suki got up. 'We'd better go in.'

Tania followed her down the corridor, hoping the class would be so busy she wouldn't have to talk to Suki again. She glanced around but saw no sign of Zac. Hadn't he finished changing yet?

The doors to the rehearsal room opened, and a young woman stuck her head out. 'You all here for the workshop? Do come in – we'll get going in a minute.'

Tania followed the others in, still wondering where Zac could have got to. 'Is it always like this?' a voice muttered in her ear, and she turned in surprise.

'Zac! I didn't see you there!'

Zac grinned sheepishly. 'Yeah, well, I'm not exactly in my usual clothes, am I?'

Tania took in the broad chest, the bare well-defined arms, and swallowed. She didn't dare look down. 'You look fine,' she said.

Zac squirmed. 'These tights go up my . . . I mean, are they *supposed* to do that?'

Tania stifled a laugh.

'Hi there.' Suki suddenly appeared at Tania's side. 'I gather you're Tania's ice-skating partner?'

'Uh – yeah,' said Zac. 'Do you know Tania?'

'Oh, we're old friends,' said Suki, with a giggle. 'I'm Suki.'

'Zac.'

'Zac – what a cool name. Is it short for Isaac?'

'Yeah.'

Tania looked at him in astonishment. She would never have guessed Zac's real name! He caught her eye and looked away in embarrassment. 'Don't tell anyone.'

'Oh, but Isaac is a great name,' said Suki, slipping her arm through Zac's. 'So strong.'

Tania felt annoyed. Who was this girl anyway? And why was she attaching herself to Zac so persuasively? And, more to the point, why wasn't Zac shaking her off?